Penny Appleton

Love, Home
At Last

A SUMMERFIELD VILLAGE
SWEET ROMANCE

Requests to publish work from this book should be sent to:
penny@pennyappleton.com

Cover and Interior Design: JD Smith Design

www.CurlUpPress.com

Dedicated to the memory of Bobby,
of all canine friends, the most loyal and true.

Chapter 1

"Lizzie!" Harry Stewart calls as he bounds onto the dance floor, a pretty girl on each arm. "Come on, Mouse. Come and dance with us!"

I clutch my glasses, wipe off the fog with the edge of my dress and then put them back on. It's so hot in here, and I can hardly see with them on, but without them, I'm lost. I'm desperate to go and dance with Harry, but I just shake my head, watching as he joins the lines on the dance floor and they step in time to the beat of the country music, wide grins on their faces. Harry doesn't know the steps well, but he joins in anyway, laughing and having a great time. He's so confident – just like he's always been.

I love to dance, and Jenna taught me the first line-dance, the one she and Dan led together. I learned that one and managed okay without glasses. It's like Scottish dancing, which I learned in Junior High. Once you know the movements, you can relax and flow with the music. But I only know that one line dance. If I jump onto the dance floor with Harry now, I'll crash into people, to my everlasting embarrassment. So much for the elegant English Maid-of-Honor. Better to stay here, hidden in the shadows. But my feet long to join the step and flow of the dancers.

1

We're all here at the Idaho ranch to celebrate the wedding of Dan and Jenna, my English brother and his gorgeous, new American wife. I'm so happy for them, but I can't help comparing myself to those around me. My nickname was 'Mouse' when Dan, Harry and I were younger. I guess it still fits because I'm small. If you were kind, you'd say I'm petite, but I like to bake and eat delicious things, and my curves are getting curvier these days. But who can resist a freshly baked coffee cake with caramelized walnuts? Or the glorious warm softness of a new loaf of bread?

I'm also mousey because of my naturally light brown hair, usually pulled back in clips or a scrunchy, a practical look for working in the kitchen or stables. But today, my hair is highlighted pale blond and hangs loosely around my shoulders. It's been beautifully cut and styled, just like Jenna's. I see her and Dan across the dance floor, her straight, blue-black hair tossing like the mane of her beautiful Appaloosa stallion, Blue, as she steps and turns, laughing over her shoulder at Dan's dancing style. She holds her white silk dress a few inches above her feet in white cowboy boots, looking every inch the rancher she has become.

As Dan's Best Man, Harry dances on her other side. He and Dan stand out in the black pants and white shirts from their wedding outfits. Their jackets, string ties, and Stetsons have all been discarded, their shirt sleeves rolled up to the elbow. Around them, family and friends wear new blue jeans and checkered shirts, or denim skirts and cowboy gear for a Western-style wedding. Greg, Jenna's dad, is out there too, dancing with his wife, Maggie, my godmother and Harry's mum. Our families are tied together in so many ways now, and it makes me smile to see everyone so happy.

But in the corner of my heart, there's an ache. Will this kind of happiness ever happen for me?

As a bridesmaid, I should probably be flirting with some of the local guys, but I've never been very confident with meeting new people, and I can't take my eyes off Harry as he twirls one of the American girls, catching her around the waist, his red-gold hair reflecting the lights. When Dan and I were growing up, Harry lived near us in Summerfield. Maggie was a single parent and had to travel with her job, so Harry stayed with us a lot. He's always been the total opposite of a mouse. He's like a young lion with his tawny hair and athletic figure, bounding with energy. Popular and fashionable, Harry has a winning smile and a different haircut every time I see him. He was an actor for a time, but now he's an international photographer, traveling the world. I just wish he could see me as someone more than Dan's little sister.

My two little half-brothers from Australia, Adam and Matt, dive through the crowd and hide behind me, interrupting my thoughts. They peep out from behind the skirt of my wine-red dress, and I grin down at them. They are still wearing identical dark blue Stetsons, which they just won't take off. With jeans, red checkered shirts, and cowboy boots, they look quite the part in this Western scene.

"Hey, guys. What's up?"

"Shhh." Matt scans the crowd in one direction, Adam in the other. "Mum's taking Ellie back, she says it's time for bed, and Dad's got to get us, too." Matt makes a face.

"We're not tired, and it's not fair." Adam looks exhausted. "We're older than Ellie, so we should stay up much later."

"Uh-oh, there's Dad. You didn't see us, right?"

"Right."

The boys disappear.

I lean against the wall of the barn and sip a root beer, the tangy fizz a welcome coolness. Then one of the guests pushes open the big doors of the barn and a cool night breeze blows through, calming me. I take a deep breath, trying to relax after a crazy day. We had a crisis earlier in the evening when Mum went missing. She has early onset

Alzheimer's disease, and it could have been a disaster. Dan and I were frantic, and we all searched for her, eventually finding her at the top of the ranch, with Jenna's stallion, Blue, watching over her. She's physically safe and well, but she's not herself anymore. My heart beats faster with the fear of losing what little we have left of her.

The musicians stop for a break, and everyone gets cold beers and sodas. Charlie, my dad, who lives in Australia and Viv, Mum's sister, come over to join me.

"How's Mum doing?"

Viv pats my arm. "Christine's sleeping, and I'll go back in an hour. It'll be time for bed by then. It's been an exciting day."

"It certainly has." Charlie takes a sip of his beer. "And we're lucky that everything worked out okay." He looks around, scanning the crowd. "I'll just finish this drink, and then I have to find the boys."

"They went past a minute ago." I grin at him. "But I didn't see them, okay?"

Charlie laughs. "Thanks, Lizzie." He pauses, then puts an arm around me. "I'm so sorry that Christine is unwell."

I lean into his hug, grateful for his support, although we are only beginning to get to know each other. Charlie and Mum separated before I was born, and he went back to Australia, not knowing that she was pregnant. After the divorce, he sent presents for my birthday and Christmas, but Mum's bitterness meant I was not allowed to visit him and his new family.

Meeting him for the first time just a few days ago was a bit traumatic, to be honest. But life is complicated, I guess. When he saw me, Charlie said that I was the spitting image of his sister, Sheila, in Perth. It hadn't been noticeable in pictures of me over the years, maybe because I don't like having my picture taken. But his words made our family real, as I don't look like anyone on Mum's side of the family.

When I was much younger and things were tough, I'd make up stories for myself, that I was someone else's baby, that the hospital made a mistake. But the paternity test nailed it. Charlie is my Dad.

I understand why he left and went back to Australia. After all, I grew up with Mum's violent mood swings. But I often sat in my little box room, wishing I had a normal family. Mum always adored Dan, but not me. But I was lucky to have loving grandparents and aunts nearby, plus dogs and horses to love, so I was okay. I like Charlie, but I don't feel comfortable calling him Dad yet, as Dan does. However, it's easy to be with him and Angelina, his second wife, my three half-siblings, the two boisterous boys and little Ellie, who is in a wheelchair.

All these new people have come into my life, and with Mum sick, it feels like change is coming. And that scares me a little.

Charlie pulls away from the hug and puts down his empty beer glass. "We need to talk about you coming to Cairns for a vacation, Lizzie. It was great to have Dan and Jenna over, and we'd like to show you some of beautiful Queensland as well."

I smile up at him. "Thanks so much. I'd love to come sometime, but after tonight's drama with Mum, I need to be at Home Farm with her. She's going to need a different level of support from now on." I push away thoughts of golden sand, blue skies, and Australian sunshine. "Hopefully, I can come sometime in the future."

"Anytime. You just let me know."

Charlie squeezes my hand, his eyes saying a lot more than his words, then heads off to look for the boys. Viv is talking to someone else now, and I stand by her side, watching the colorful scene in front of me as my mind drifts back to the farm.

I'm not academic like Dan and I always loved being

there with the ponies and our other animals. After high school, I took over managing a lot of the practicalities. These days, I'm the cook and housekeeper for Mum, and also her caregiver. A sudden wave of guilt washes over me at the thoughts of escaping. I'm not Mum's favorite, but she needs me now, more than ever.

Harry moves through the crowd toward me, one camera in his hand, another slung around his neck, a transformation from party boy to photographer. He corrals guests together, cracking jokes to make them pose and smile.

"Great pictures for the wedding album, everyone. Jenna and Dan will love these."

He turns toward Viv and me, focusing the lens. "Here are two of my favorite people. Smile, Viv." He pops his head up. "Take your glasses off, Lizzie. They're all fogged up."

I remove them quickly and stuff them in my small purse as Viv puts her arm around me. We both smile at the camera. Harry fires off several shots and then pauses, looking at me, his head tipped to one side.

A flicker of something flows between us in the intensity of his gaze. It's as if he suddenly sees me through his camera, someone more than the mouse he remembers from our childhood. He checks the camera and grins. "Beautiful."

Dan calls from the bar, holding up a bottle of whiskey and two glasses. "Harry, get over here!"

Harry smiles at us. "Sorry ladies, gotta go. Best Man duty calls."

He starts to walk away but then turns back, looking at me with a puzzled gaze. I clutch my purse, a shield against my pounding heart as I meet his eyes before he turns away again.

Viv shakes her head. "That Harry, such a charmer, especially when he's holding that camera. A girl on every continent and an allergic reaction to commitment, no doubt."

Her words echo in my mind as I watch Harry at the bar

with Dan, best friends reminiscing about times past as my brother begins a new chapter in his life. But what about mine?

* * *

Next morning, those of us staying at the ranch house gather out front to wave goodbye to the newlyweds as they head off on their honeymoon road trip. Harry is at one end of the veranda, clutching a mug of black coffee. His hair is ruffled, his shirt buttoned up wrong, as he leans against the wooden rail. He smiles at me and starts to come over. He looks as if he's about to say something, but then Jenna and Dan come out of the kitchen door, bags in hand, kissing everyone goodbye, followed by Greg and Maggie.

"Safe journey, have fun!"

Everyone kisses and hugs and finally, Dan drives off, Jenna waving from her window as the Jeep pulls away. All the ranch dogs race after them, barking like crazy. When the dust settles, Greg looks out at the yard and the barn beyond. It looks like the aftermath of a great party. He takes a deep breath.

"Anyone for pancakes?"

As everyone heads back inside again, Harry comes over.

"I'm heading off now, Mouse, but I'll be in and out of Heathrow over the next couple of months and staying in Summerfield for some of it. Mum says I can leave some gear at Square Cottage to save me lugging it to and from Edinburgh. Shall we meet up with Clair and have a drink at the Potlatch, like the old days?"

My heart skips a beat. Clair is my best friend, and when we were teenagers, we often used to meet up with Harry and other kids from the village. I can't help my wide smile. "I'd love to. Let me know when you're back."

He leans in, and for a moment, I think he's going to kiss me.

I lift my head, and he turns his face to kiss me on the cheek. A very chaste, brotherly kiss.

My heart sinks as he walks away and I head in for pancakes, ready to drown my sorrows in maple syrup, kicking myself for thinking there was something different in his gaze last night. It's time I stopped pining after Harry Stewart, but he's always been the one, and he's a hard habit to break.

I fell in love with Harry when I was seven. It was my birthday. He and Dan were ten and Harry gave me a gift of colored pens. After tea, when we went out to play, he dared me to jump off the hay bales in the barn. I was always desperate to hang out with him and Dan, to do the exciting things that they did.

Mum had strictly forbidden us to play in the barn as it was stacked to the roof with winter fodder for our animals. Nowadays, we have hay bales like big balls wrapped in black plastic, but back then, brick-shaped bales of hay were stacked on different levels right up to the roof of the big barn. It looked like three Olympic diving boards. The two lower levels were fine. We all flew through the air, shrieking with laughter, landing in a pile of loose hay. But when we climbed to the very top, I was scared. The boys jumped straight off, but I stood up there looking down at the ground so far away. Dan called up. "Climb down, Lizzie, it's too high for you."

I leaned right out to see Harry dancing in the soft hay pile, way down below. He beckoned. "Come on, Lizzie, you can do it!"

I trusted him, so I jumped.

But somehow, I twisted in the air. There was a crunch as I hit the ground, my right arm crushed beneath me, as my breath was knocked from my lungs. Pain shot through me and tears welled up as Dan freaked out. "That was your fault, Harry. Now you've got to go and tell Mum."

Harry knelt in the hay, holding my other hand, his brilliant blue eyes full of regret. "I'm so sorry, Lizzie. I thought it would be okay. You were so brave to jump."

Mum was furious with me when we made it back into the house. "I've told you time and time again, Lizzie. Stay away from Daniel and Harry. They don't want you, and now look what you've done."

Harry helped me into the Land Rover and fastened my seatbelt. In the hospital, Mum stayed angry, pacing up and down. My arm hurt a lot when they put it in a cast, but Harry distracted me with silly stories, his arm around my shoulders. To him, I was just Dan's little sister, but to me, he was my knight in shining armor. I have longed for his arms around me ever since.

Chapter 2

A few days later, I'm heading back home, ready to get things back to normal after the trip away. Mum needs a medical checkup after her episode in Idaho, so Viv has taken her to stay in Oxford with her and Sid. I push Harry firmly from my mind and focus on all the things that need to be ready for her return. While we've been away, my best friend Clair has been feeding the dogs and ponies, and I'm looking forward to a grand reunion with all of them.

The taxi drops me at Home Farm with my bags. I only had one bag when I left, but Maggie took me shopping, as she always does when we get together. I don't have many opportunities to wear beautiful clothes in Summerfield, but it's sweet of her to care. For now, I'll be hanging them in my closet and changing back into jeans and sweatshirts for work. I key in the security number and the big gate slides gently across. Up by the pony barn, I see our two black Labradors turn at the distinctive sound. They race toward me, ears flapping, barking with excitement.

"Come on then, lovely boys."

I sit down on the bench by Dan's studio before Jester reaches me. Sometimes his enthusiasm can be overwhelming, and if he hits at full speed, you're liable to go flying. I smile to remember Mum roaring at him, "I swear, Jester, if I didn't know for certain you are Pluto's pedigree son, I wouldn't believe it!"

Jester arrives and tries to sit on my lap, his laughing face telling me he's glad I'm home. I stroke his head and push him down.

"Yes, I missed you, too. Now sit, Jester."

He has the most wonderful, glossy black coat, but also a wild tail that whips your legs and can sweep anything off low surfaces. Most Labradors stop chewing things after a year, but Jester is now four and still chews anything he can get his paws on. He's picked up a gift for me on the way down the slope and drops it by my feet.

"Thank you." I gingerly accept the torn gardening glove. "I suppose this is from your retrieving ancestry and could be a fine duck?"

Jester wags his tail so fast he's almost bent double in the middle, just as Pluto reaches us at last. He's old, almost twelve, and his legs are shaky with arthritis. He sits down next to me with a sigh and rests his beautiful head on my knee. I stroke it gently, noticing that his muzzle is now entirely gray.

"Dear old Pluto." I gaze into the eyes I've loved since he was a plump and adorable puppy. "How are you doing, old mate?" I stand up. "Right, lads, let's get my bags indoors, and then do the pony feeds."

It's good to be back, and the dogs join me on a quick inspection tour. I grew up being on my own a lot, and animals are my best friends. Granddad Arthur, Mum and Viv's dad, gave Home Farm to Mum when Dan was born. Dan and I have been so lucky to grow up here with Mum's herd of thoroughbred Welsh ponies, the dogs, barn cats, and chickens.

I cross the gravel driveway to the front of our Elizabethan farmhouse. It's a long building, built of warm, russet bricks in squares between the black, painted beams. All the windows are original, with small, diamond-shaped panes. A stone lion sits in splendid isolation by the front door. There's an air of expectancy, everything holding its breath, waiting for Mum to come home. But even when she's physically present these days, I guess she's not really here anymore.

The immaculate flowerbeds are bursting with blue delphiniums, and I notice that the contract gardener has been in to mow the lawn. It all looks perfect for a game of croquet, accompanied by afternoon tea served with homemade scones, my strawberry jam, and clotted cream. But we haven't had a tournament for several years now. Mum used to glide effortlessly through a gilded world of colorful people, but it all ended with Alzheimer's disease. Her moods have always been unpredictable, but now she often doesn't recognize people she once knew, so they don't come over anymore.

My phone buzzes. It's Clair.

"Hey, you! Thanks for covering everything over here while we've been away. I'm just going up to the field to bring in the ponies."

"I'm so glad you're back. I can't wait to see you and hear all about the wedding. I'm just finishing up, and then I'll be free."

"I could come over there ... but guess who I just met in the village?" Clair's voice has that edge of gossip to it.

"No idea, who?"

"Harry. He's staying at Square Cottage until tomorrow. He's looking a bit gorgeous, isn't he? I told him we were getting together and he suggested meeting at the Potlatch. What do you think?"

I'm surprised to hear he's back so soon and, of course, I want to see him. But I try not to sound too keen. "Um, okay."

Clair laughs. She knows me so well. "See you there in an hour. I'll call Harry and tell him."

I give the dogs rawhide treats to chew while I check the house. Dan and I were young when Granddad showed us the Deed of Purchase, a huge crested parchment, granting the land in 1601. The house was built in the same year, but now we have the wonders of central heating and a beautiful new kitchen. This is my domain, and I'm looking forward to doing some cooking tomorrow. I love this house when it's filled with the smells of home.

The heavy living room curtains are closed against the night, and I switch the side lamps on to give it a warmer feel. It's so familiar in here, with comfortable couches against the walls and old Persian carpets on the stone-tiled floor. Mum has hosted many parties here, and it's full of happy memories. Strange to be here on my own right now.

I tread softly on the deep blue carpet between Mum's oil paintings of famous horses and climb the main staircase, negotiating the narrow, wooden stairs to my room in the attic. This was my sanctuary when Mum was on the warpath, the old servant's quarters. It's not much to look at, but no one else comes up here. I should probably move downstairs to be closer to her bedroom now, but old habits die hard. I even miss her shouting at me.

The reality of Mum's illness suddenly hits me, because we had some happy times here as well. Tears prickle my eyes. Will this old house ever ring to the sound of laughter again? I shake my head. I really need to get out of here and see some friendly faces.

I pull on comfortable old jeans and a faded sweatshirt then jump back down the stairs. The dogs wait by the back door as I find my gumboots and an old coat. "Come on boys. Let's go find those ponies."

I mix the feeds in the tack room next to the barn. It was built at the same time as the house and has giant rounded cobbles in the floor. I love the way they dip in all sorts of odd places where the land beneath has moved over the centuries. But I'm less pleased to look up and notice a patch of rain-damaged ceiling. Another item on the list of chores for tomorrow.

Clair filled the racks with sweet hay after she let the ponies out this morning, so I chop apple from our orchard and carrot pieces from the garden into a bucket. Whistling a happy tune, I walk to the top paddock with Pluto and Jester to where our beautiful Welsh Mountain ponies jostle at the gate. They line up as Mum has taught them, intelligent faces expectant, eager to come in for the night. I give out treats of carrots and apples as I check them over, stroking a muzzle here, patting a neck there and pulling tangles of dry thorn from their manes.

"Okay, you all look fine. Off you go." I open the gate and one by one, they walk through it and down to the barn. "Steady, Dolores."

The gray mare is heavily in foal and a bit of a kicker at the best of times. When she landed a kick on me before, I was in agony for a week. As I shut the gate behind us, I give her one of the last two small apples, then bite into the other myself. It's crunchy and juicy sweet, a taste of home.

Back in the warm barn, I check the water, listening to the happy sound of ponies munching hay.

"I'll be in again to see you before bed."

I walk out and lock the doors, then quickly feed the dogs and head back upstairs to shower and change. My heart is beating faster now. I'm looking forward to catching up with Clair, but I'm also seeing Harry tonight, and I can't keep the smile off my face.

I dress quickly in new, fitted jeans, a pretty sweater, and low-heeled, black boots that have never touched a yard. I add some light makeup, barely visible under my glasses, then I let my hair out of its ponytail and brush it to fall, silky blond, onto my shoulders. I normally drive the old truck, but tonight, I take Mum's red Range Rover and park it carefully outside The Potlatch Inn.

It's the only pub in Summerfield and the social center where most people meet. There's been some kind of hostelry here since medieval times, but this building is of deep gray stone and dates from the seventeenth century. Warm light from within the bustling pub illuminates the wooden sign swinging gently in the wind above the gate. It shows the potlatch, a round gray boulder, sitting on a green field surrounded by hills. A glimpse into Summerfield's past when potlatches were gathered and split to form the roof tiles still found on most of the old cottages, including Maggie's cottage next door … where Harry is right this minute.

I look toward the cottage, biting my lip as I consider going over just as Clair swings into the parking lot in her green Summerfield Stables Jeep. She waves enthusiastically, her brown curly hair bouncing around her smiling face and laughing eyes.

She parks and gets out of the car, bending to hug me as she's so much taller. "So glad you're back."

"Missed you, too."

She pulls away and looks at me. "You look great. New clothes, a tan, and I love your hair. How did the wedding go?"

"It was amazing and lovely to see Dan and Jenna so happy."

We walk together toward the pub door. "I can't wait to see the photos. It's cold out here, let's get inside."

Clair is my best friend. She came to live in Summerfield with her grandparents, Ted and May, when she was thirteen. We bonded over a shared love of horses, and we've been close ever since.

I push open the door, and the familiar smell of roasting meat mingled with warm fruit and cinnamon fill the air. The Potlatch is one of the best places to eat in Summerfield, with home-cooked food available every day, and tonight, it's busy with locals and a few out-of-towners. The music is low, enough to relax and hear each other talk. I exhale and begin to relax. Clair and I have been coming here for years, and it's good to be around people after the emptiness of the farmhouse. We grab a drink and then sit in one of the corner booths, the oak benches polished to a shine by generations of people.

Clair frowns as she looks around. "I thought Kyle would be here."

I suppress a groan. Her current boyfriend was our farrier for a while, working with the ponies at one time. But he wasn't gentle, and he didn't love the animals as we did. He never did anything wrong as such, but it was obvious in his manner. He didn't last long at Home Farm, and he is not one of my favorite people. "How are things with him?"

"He's driving me crazy." She shakes her head and takes a sip of her drink. "I'm not sure how much longer it's going to last."

Clair always tries to be cheerful but, like me, she has her black moments. Kyle is totally hot, but unfortunately, he knows it. There's little choice for dates in Summerfield, and living in the country means slim pickings for Clair and me on the dating front.

"It's so hard to meet anyone if you don't work in town and don't like going to the clubs in Oxford." Clair stares gloomily into her glass. "This village is like a soap opera. Drama, drama, drama, about something or other. But where's the romantic stuff from TV, Liz? It never seems to happen to either of us."

I laugh and raise my glass in a toast. "Then here's to being happy old maids."

We giggle, and Clair moves a wooden stool nearer and puts her feet up. "Oh, it's good to have a moment to relax. I've been on these all day."

Clair's Granddad Ted is in his eighties now, and her

Grandma May passed away recently, so Clair runs the Summerfield Stables herself, offering livery and grazing. She's also a qualified riding instructor and gives lessons in the indoor and outdoor arenas. Her work life seems pretty sorted, but her love life is a mess – just like mine.

She sighs. "While you were away, our new Stables Manager, Robert, arrived. Granddad can't do much now, and I just can't manage on my own, so it's great to have a new hand on deck."

"What's he like?"

"He was an officer in the Mounted Police but retired after a fall during a riot at a football game. He still walks with a limp from the injury. The Riding with Challenges Program recommended him."

I know how much the program means to Clair. She offers people with physical or emotional disabilities an opportunity to work with her gentle horses and learn to ride. I think of little Ellie, disabled and living in Australia, learning to ride with the help of a saddle that Jenna designed. Maybe the same type of thing would help some of Clair's students, too. I like the idea of weaving our communities together across the oceans.

The door creaks open. I look up, hoping it will be Harry. But Kyle walks in, a hulking figure in his black leather jacket, with broad shoulders and tight jeans that sit well on his muscular body.

He heads to the bar. Clair gets up. "I won't be a minute."

She walks over and leans in to kiss him on the cheek, and they talk in low tones. I turn away and look around, suddenly noticing that there's new art on the walls of the pub. Selena, who owns the place with her husband, Tom, is great about supporting local artists and changes the pictures regularly. These are simple, framed watercolors of the Summerfield area, with light-washed greens of the hills and the colors of autumn in the leaves on the trees in the foreground. I turn around to look at the ones behind me. The closest is a horse running through the fields, the artist catching its powerful movement in simple lines.

It shocks me for a moment because I used to sketch like this, but I never took it forward to anything more, and I haven't sketched in ages. When I mentioned going to art school a few years back, Mum scoffed and said I wasn't good enough, and besides, she needed me to run the farm, and wasn't that good enough for me?

Maybe it was good enough, but seeing these pictures makes my fingers itch for my pencils and my sketchbook.

The door opens with a creak, and I look up again.

This time, Harry walks in.

Chapter 3

He doesn't see me at first, his face turned away in profile as he scans the room. Then he turns, and his blue eyes light up as he smiles and waves at me. It's like the sun has come out, and I can't help my wide smile as he walks over and kisses me on the cheek.

"Great to see you again so soon, Lizzie, and it's good to be back in Summerfield after too long away."

"Not so much changes around here, as you can see." I point toward Clair at the bar. "Just like old times."

"How's your mum?" Harry's blue eyes are kind and interested, not like some people who ask but really don't want to know. I take off my glasses and clean them until I can speak without getting tearful.

"She's not good. Viv is looking after her in Oxford until the specialist completes the tests while I look after Home Farm. To be honest, the next bit is going to be difficult."

"I'm so sorry." He squeezes my hand. "Remember to look after yourself as well. You can't have your whole life revolving around your mum, after all."

His words resonate deep inside because part of me wants to shout 'yes, I need to be free' and the other part is guilty at wishing things were different. Guilt and duty and love all mingled up inside. I change the subject before the tears come.

"Do you remember when I used to sketch?"

Harry nods. "Of course. When Dan and I used to race around the yard, you would sit in the corner with your sketchbook. You were always drawing ponies and dogs. Are you still doing art?"

I shake my head. "There's been no time. It takes a lot to run the farm especially as Mum has gone downhill. I've been baking a lot, selling artisan bread at the market, but to be honest, my heart's not really in that anymore."

He reaches out and squeezes my hand. "It sounds like you've got some thinking to do, Mouse. Let me know if you need anything. After all, now Dan's moved away, I'm like your older brother."

His words give me a sinking feeling. He still sees me as that little girl in the corner of the yard.

"Hey, Harry!" A man shouts from the doorway. Harry stands up.

"Sorry, Lizzie, I've got a meeting with this photographer friend and have to arrange transport for tomorrow. Take care of yourself. I'll say bye to Clair as I go."

He bends to give me a brotherly kiss, waves at the man by the door and then walks across to speak to Clair, before heading out into the night.

Clair and Kyle seem to be arguing. She slams her glass down on the bar then stalks back over.

"I'm over men." She sits down. "How about you? Still drooling over the unobtainable Harry Stewart?"

I make a face at her.

"You can fool everyone else, Lizzie, but you can't fool me."

"Then thank goodness it's only you. When he smiles, I feel like ... Oh, whatever. Harry lives in Edinburgh now when he's not jet-setting all over the world doing photo shoots."

Clair leans in. "You're looking thoughtful, though. What is it?"

I point up at the watercolor of the horse above me. "I was just thinking that I haven't sketched in so long and I asked Harry if he remembered me doing it. He used to encourage me a lot – at least that's how I remember it. One day he found me hiding from Mum in a sweet chestnut tree between our farm and Potlatch Wood. He didn't tell a soul, not even Dan, but he brought me sketchpads and pencils. He even found an old leather briefcase to put them in and a plastic sheet for when it rained."

"That's kind. That must have been before I came because you've never mentioned it before."

I nod. "I don't even think he remembers. Anyway, he's off to a photo shoot in Florida soon. I can just picture those hot models in bikinis while we're shivering here in winter."

Clair grins. "We could always muck out the stables together in hot pants and crop tops. Now that would be a helluva photo shoot!"

We burst into laughter, and I'm suddenly cheerful again.

"Harry has his life, and we have ours. I need to head back now. So much to do and I'm going to have a grand morning baking before Mum comes back tomorrow afternoon, to celebrate everything being back to normal. Would you and Ted like a cake?"

"Oh, yes please. Your lemon drizzle loaf is his all-time favorite."

We get up and link arms, best friends against the world, and head out into the night. Who needs Harry Stewart, anyway?

I drive home, my mind filled with all the things I have to get sorted out to make the place shipshape for Mum coming home. I'm expecting to be alone in the house, but as the gate slides open at Home Farm, I see Viv's car parked next to the garage.

Strange. I wasn't expecting her tonight.

I get out of the car to a happy greeting by the dogs, then hurry around to the back door. Viv sits up at the breakfast counter in the kitchen, her face crumpled with anxiety. It must be about Mum, and a feeling of dread rises inside me.

"What is it? Why didn't you call to say you were coming over? I was only at the Potlatch. I'd have come straight back."

I bustle around, put the kettle on, anything to postpone the moment when she will tell me why she's here.

"Tea? Cake? Anything?"

Viv shakes her head and pats the stool next to her. "Sit down a minute, love."

I perch on the edge of one of the stools and she takes my hand. "Uh-oh, this looks serious."

She nods. "I'm sorry, Lizzie, but it is. The hospital appointment was traumatic. Christine is often in a world of her own now and sometimes doesn't even recognize me. But today she screamed and fought everyone when they tried to examine her. Her dementia has moved into a more violent phase."

"But she'll be fine here with me, I'm sure of it. I'm used to her moods. She's always had them, and I know when to stay out of her way."

Viv shakes her head. "Her condition is getting to the stage where we can't manage her safely. The specialist says that Christine needs full-time professional care in a dedicated dementia facility. He went over everything offered by a place called Green Acres. It's near our house ... but it's expensive." Viv's eyes well up with tears. "Sid's been working on the numbers. I'm so sorry, Lizzie, but Christine owns this land and the house. I'm her Executor and I have her financial Power of Attorney. We need to sell Home Farm to pay her expenses."

Her words wash over me. I hear them, but I can't seem to understand what she's saying. I stand up and look around the kitchen. It's always been my haven, the place I've created food that made even Mum smile. I look out at the yard and in the gloom, I see the barn where the ponies are safely in for the night. This is my home. I can't even consider losing it.

I turn back to Viv. "But … but what about the ponies?"

"The farmer in Wales, the one who bought the stallion last year, would like to buy them."

I nod. He was a good man. The horses liked him. "Okay, but what about the dogs? Mum needs them."

"We'll take them to live with us so they can visit her. She recognizes them even though she can't remember their names."

I wipe my eyes, realizing there's only one question left.

"But what about me? What am I supposed to do?"

Viv gets up and comes over to hug me. "I'm sorry, love. Sid and I think of you as a daughter, but we don't have room for you at ours. You could rent somewhere here, maybe get a job at the Country Club or the Stables with Clair. Or maybe it's time to think about moving on and doing something new with your life. You're young, Lizzie. You have so many options." Viv sighs and shakes her head. "But Christine has no more options, and our parents told me to look after her, and I'll always do that. We need the money from Home Farm to finance her future care. I hope there'll be some left for you eventually, but we have to sell."

A yawning sinkhole opens up in front of me as her words become real. A great wave of panic sweeps over me as I realize that my time at Home Farm is over. Will I ever find a home again?

Chapter 4

Viv rubs her eyes, the frown lines deepening around them and I notice the black shadows beneath. This is hard for all of us. "I'm tired now, so I'm going to go home. Will you be alright?"

I nod as she carries on.

"We're transferring Christine to Green Acres tomorrow at lunchtime when she's discharged from the hospital. Then a real estate agent is meeting Sid and me here at three to look over the property for the valuation. I know this is a big shock for you, Lizzie. You're welcome to be here, but if you choose not to be, I understand. Things need to move fast because of the financial situation, but we'll talk some more tomorrow night, okay?"

"Okay." I can't think of anything more to say as we walk out to Viv's car and hug goodbye.

Tires crunch on the gravel, the gate opens and closes again. The sound of the car fades into the distance, and silence surges back into the yard.

My mind is reeling and tears well up as I look around at the only home I've ever known. I sit on the bench and Pluto comes over, nudging my leg with his nose. "Oh, lovely boy, what am I going to do?"

I wrap my arms around him and cry, letting his warmth comfort me, but it isn't enough. I need to talk to Dan, but he's still away on his honeymoon, and I don't want to ruin their happiness. He can't do anything right now, anyway. Clair will be sleeping, exhausted and recharging her batteries for tomorrow. She has enough to cope with right now, so I don't want to wake her. There is nothing anyone can do to help.

Then I remember that Harry is still at Square Cottage until tomorrow. He spent so many summers at Home Farm, I know he'll understand. Maybe I do need a big brother right now, after all.

I pull out my phone and text him.

Harry, Are you awake? It's urgent. Can I come over?

His message comes back quickly.

Of course, I'm up editing photos. Come over.

I take my old truck this time and park it by the garage at Square Cottage. It's perfectly square with a big chimney-pot on the top of a roof covered in the heritage potlatch tiles of the area. Smoke curls out of the chimney and a soft light shines out from one of the downstairs windows. It looks so welcoming. Harry opens the back door as I walk down the path.

"What's up, Lizzie?" He sees my face. "Oh, you've been crying. Is it your mum? Come in."

I nod, but my words are choked by tears. He takes my hand and leads me through to the kitchen. It's toasty warm from the big black Aga stove, an old-fashioned range with two shiny silver lids on top covering circular hotplates. Harry lifts the top of one and puts a kettle on top, boiling water for tea.

I take off my coat and boots, then climb on a tall stool

at the breakfast bar. I rest my elbows on the top, fighting to hold back my tears.

"Viv was there when I got back from the pub." My voice breaks a little, and I take a deep breath. "Mum needs to go into a specialist care facility, and Home Farm must be sold to pay for it. I'm going to lose my home."

Then I can't hold back enormous gulps of heartbroken sobbing. I take off my glasses and put them on the counter-top. Harry comes over and wraps his arms around me, rubbing my back as I cry. He rocks me gently in his arms, and I rest my face against his chest. My tears soak his sweater.

"Oh Lizzie, I'm so sorry."

I cling to him, my dear friend from the past until I my sobs subside a little. I pull back from him and blow my nose. "Our house, Harry, and the yard, the bluebell wood. All the childhood places where we grew up, they'll be gone forever. Dan will be devastated."

"We had such good times there, that's for sure."

He hands me my tea. I take a sip, and the warm drink soothes me a little. I explain what Viv told me and the plans for the valuation. How fast everything is suddenly moving.

"So what are you going to do?"

I shrug. "I really don't know, but I don't think I can stay here. The whole village will be talking about us, and maybe it's time I got out of Summerfield." His face is concerned, his blue eyes looking closely at me, and I'm suddenly aware of my puffy skin and runny nose. "Just let me go wash my face a minute, then maybe we can talk some more."

I go to the bathroom to wash my face, and when I return, Harry is pouring more strong English breakfast tea into our mugs. He looks over at me, and there is a change in his expression, a thoughtfulness in his eyes. "I have an idea that could possibly help."

"Please, anything." I sit back down at the breakfast bar.

"Do you remember The Warehouse, the student place where Dan and I lived in Edinburgh?"

Images of a pretty awful student flat flash through my mind. "I think Dan might have shown me some photos once. Aren't you still living there?"

Harry nods. "It's my base, but I travel a lot, so I'm hardly there. It belongs to my dad. He bought a run-down area with old warehouses near the old docks in Leith. He reckoned it would be a key development site in the future, but the future was a long time coming. Meanwhile, to bring in some income from the investment, he had the biggest building converted into affordable housing."

I don't know where Harry is going with this, so I sip my tea and listen. I'm feeling calmer now, crying always helps get the immediate stress out and sharing the problem with him is helping too, like it always did in the past.

"When I graduated, I took over from Dad as the landlord. An old friend from college, Anna, has been the custodian. The job pays no wage, but it's only part-time and comes with a free apartment. Anna is an interior designer, and she's starting to do really well, so she wants to give up the custodian job. There's an empty apartment on the top floor of The Warehouse, and I've been looking for someone suitable to be the new custodian and live up there."

I'm confused for a moment, then his words make sense. "You're offering me a job?"

Harry shrugs. "I know it's not perfect, but if you want it, Lizzie, you'd be welcome to the job and the apartment. If it helps you, of course. It's nothing much to look after the place, certainly after what you've been used to on the farm. There are excellent art courses in Edinburgh, and you could get a part-time job and work toward your college degree at the same time. It's just an idea. Take some time to think about it."

His words are a lifeline, and suddenly I'm not sinking into despair anymore. "Harry, I don't need to think about it. Yes... Yes, please. I'd love the job and the apartment."

He raises an eyebrow. "Are you sure? It's not perfect by any means."

I jump up and go to hug him, this time without being a weeping mess. "But it's a start. It means that I can leave Summerfield with my head held high. I'd have a job, a place to live and maybe even a chance to go to college."

"I travel almost every second week, usually out of the country, so I'm not there a lot. Are you okay with that?"

"Of course. When can I start? I'd love to get out of here before people start viewing the property and I can get the animals taken care of before I go."

Harry collects our mugs and washes them up in the sink. "I'll call Anna first thing in the morning and tell her to expect you, so whenever you're ready. I've got several back-to-back assignments lined up, but Anna will show you around and explain the job." He pauses and looks up. "It's a good deal for me too, Lizzie. I trust you with the place, and I know you'll do a great job." He meets my eyes. "And we might even get to spend some more time together."

His words could mean anything, but right now, I'm excited about a new start. Harry walks me back to the truck and closes my door when I'm behind the wheel. "I'll email all the details. See you in Edinburgh, Mouse."

As I drive away, it feels as if my life is a line of dominoes. One has been pushed over and has knocked the next. Life can really change that fast.

* * *

The next few days are nonstop. I tell Clair everything on the phone and she immediately offers me a job at The Stables and a room to stay in.

"You know you can stay as long as you like, Lizzie."

I hear the concern in her voice, and I'm grateful to have

such a great friend. "Thanks, but it's time to leave. I need to get away, and Edinburgh will be just a stop gap, I'm sure."

"You'll come back to visit, won't you?"

"Of course."

She pauses for a moment and then says, "And you be careful of Harry Stewart. Don't let him break your heart, Lizzie. Find yourself a hot Scot while you're up there."

We laugh together and promise to speak soon.

Viv and I pack up the house. The big furniture will be sold at auction, since neither Dan nor I want it. Our personal stuff and Mum's things will go into storage for now, waiting until we have somewhere to move them to. Dan wanted to come back to help, but I told him to stay with Jenna. They are making a new home together now, and this is part of his old life. They'll come back and visit Mum in a few months, but I'm feeling stronger now, and even excited about a new start.

The dogs are settled in with Viv and Sid, so even though I'll miss them, I'll see them again when I visit. But I'm desolate as the ponies are loaded into their horse trailers for the journey to Wales. I check their hay nets and water for the last time, then stand and watch as the cavalcade goes out of the gates and disappears down the lane.

All that I love has now gone from Home Farm. It's not my home anymore.

I get my bags and head into Oxford to say goodbye to Mum before leaving from there on the train. The Green Acres facility is pleasant, painted in shades of calming sky blue and sea-green. It smells of flowers, not antiseptic like a hospital. Mum is in one of the common areas, and she seems calm as I enter. She sits in an armchair facing long windows that overlook a rose garden. A big television is on quietly in the corner, but she stares outside, her face slack, a shell of the feisty woman she used to be. I sit next to her, and we watch the birds together. She doesn't seem to register that I'm there. The nurse said she had recently had her medication. After an hour sitting quietly, I take her hand and squeeze it. "Bye, Mum. I'll be back soon to visit you."

She doesn't even turn her head.

I walk out into the bright, sunny day, wiping the tears from my cheeks. I hate to see her like that. I hate to leave her here. Love and guilt wage their war inside me again, but at least she is safe, her sister is close, and I need to get on with my life.

* * *

The next morning, I board the train for Edinburgh, and as the gentle hills of the south of England fade into the distance, I put my sadness in a box inside and shut the lid, looking ahead to the craggy mountains of Scotland and a new start.

Hours later, on a bus to Leith from the center of Edinburgh, I gaze out at my new city. I had expected modern office buildings, but the streets are lined with tall tenement blocks, five stories high and built of granite. They have rows of chimney pots along the roofs and small windows. It's drizzling and feels grim after the green fields of Oxfordshire. I huddle into my coat as the doors of the bus open and close. Dan told me that the weather could sometimes be glorious in Edinburgh, but that it was frequently wet with strong winds sweeping up the Firth of Forth from the North Sea. I expect I'll get used to it, but there is a voice of doubt in my head that sounds like my mother. *You're useless, Lizzie. You'll never amount to anything.*

I push the thought firmly away. The Scottish accents of the women around me sound just like Maggie, and she doesn't think I'm useless. Harry doesn't think I'm useless, either, or he wouldn't have offered me this job – even if it is just caretaker for some student apartments.

The bus terminates in Leith, and I step out into the darkness, shrugging into my backpack and dragging my big bag on wheels. I walk tall and keep repeating to myself. *I am Lizzie Martin, free and moving on. I am Lizzie Martin, free and moving on.*

I pass empty buildings and a few local shops, following directions on my phone. Some of the houses are boarded up, and in the gloom, I see homeless people huddled in doorways, blankets wrapped around them against the cold. The street is littered with cigarette butts, beer cans, and junk food packets. Harry mentioned that the area was run-down, but I'm starting to feel unsafe out here.

But then Summerfield is nothing like the gritty city. For a moment, I feel like running back to the station, getting on the train and heading south again. But I take a deep breath and march on. I have to give my new start a chance.

I walk along a side street, then another and finally reach a run-down industrial building. My heart sinks as I stop and peer at my phone. It's the right place. A street lamp lights three grimy steps leading to a front entrance littered with trash. The lower windows are all boarded up and covered in graffiti. It smells of stale beer. Can this really be The Warehouse, my new home?

Chapter 5

I take a deep breath and press the bell marked #3. After a few moments a voice, that of a Scottish woman, calls from somewhere above me.

"Hello, is that Lizzie?"

"Yes." It comes out as a whisper. I clear my throat and call loudly. "Yes, I'm Lizzie Martin."

"Go around the back and press my bell there. Then, come on up."

I carry my bags around the corner to find an expanse of dark wasteland stretching across to buildings on the other side. Lights shine along the path to a small parking lot. What a relief! On this side of The Warehouse, there are clean concrete steps leading up to double doors painted a soft, sky-blue color.

I press the bell, the door lock buzzes and I push it open to find a dimly lit hallway with a flight of stone stairs. The walls are painted a shiny leaf-green, and there's no elevator. The front door closes slowly on a spring as I start to climb, hauling my bags up. I concentrate on each step, so the weight doesn't send me tumbling back down again.

At the top of the next flight of stairs, a woman stands smiling down at me. She looks a little older than me, and her African braided hair ends in a mass of beautiful glass beads. She's warmly dressed in a pair of fleecy purple sweat pants with several different colored sweaters, one on top of the other. It clearly gets cold here.

"Hi Lizzie, I'm Anna MacDonald. We spoke on the phone." We shake hands. "Welcome to The Warehouse – or the madhouse, either will do!" She beckons me into her apartment. "I met your brother Dan once, but he left to go teaching in London before I moved in. Donal has his apartment now. Tea? Coffee? Sorry about that disgusting door by the footpath. We never use it. I forgot that you'd be walking from the bus stop so it would be the first bit you'd see. We don't clean that entrance, so drunks find somewhere else to sleep on a Saturday night."

I can't help smiling at Anna's enthusiastic words, and it's great to have such a warm welcome after the initial shock of the environment outside. By the time Anna has made tea and shown me around her apartment, she's said so many funny things to make me laugh, I'm sure that we're going to be good friends.

Her living room is something from a designer magazine. The walls are painted the palest hazy cappuccino, and the furniture is minimal, all stark shapes in stainless steel. In contrast, there are soft wool rugs in shades of blue and cream on pale, polished floorboards. The couches have indigo cushions and throws. There are spotlights everywhere, and it's lovely and warm compared to the stairwell.

"Anna, this is stunning!"

She smiles. "It's taken some time to get it like this, but it's my home, and I like it."

Half the room is set up as a work area with a big-screen desktop computer and design tables with swatches of fabric laid out upon it. The wall behind is covered with sketches and neat, printed design layouts. Her work in progress is beautiful, and I feel the artist in me rising as I look around. Could I make somewhere as cozy as this for myself?

"This is the kitchen area," Anna continues the tour. "That door leads to my bedroom and bathroom. It's a bit of a mess in there as I'm storing stuff for a friend temporarily. Your apartment upstairs has the same layout as mine, and Harry's and Donal's are the same. Floor one has six smaller units for students and Duncan, the owner and Harry's dad, had the ground floor rooms boarded up for security. He also rebuilt the fire escape at the back, so we have an exit in an emergency. Speaking of fire, there's no smoking in the building and one of the things you have to do as custodian is stop the students from sitting out there and smoking."

She points through a half-glazed exit door opening onto darkness and the wide iron steps attached to the building going up and down. "The students also tend to put their bikes and piles of junk here, but it must be kept clear. Not just for their safety but we also get random inspections from the Council Fire Officers. There's a massive fine if we don't comply with the regulations."

After we finish our tea, Anna helps me with my bags, and as we climb, she points to the door on the fourth landing. "That's Harry's apartment, but he comes and goes a lot. I sometimes don't see him for weeks, but he texts if there is anything we need to know about the building."

We puff to the top landing, and I bend forward, hands on my thighs to breathe deeply. I can feel my heart hammering against my ribs. "I thought I was fit from all the yard work I've done, but obviously it doesn't help with climbing stairs!"

Anna laughs as she unlocks the door. "You won't have to waste money on joining a gym. You've got your own Stairmaster right here." She reaches around the doorframe to switch on the lights and stands aside, indicating that I should go in first. "And you have the most spectacular view from up here."

I step into an empty living room as big as our main room

at Home Farm. It's stark under neon strip lights, the white paint on the walls grubby from years of use. The big windows look out onto a vast blackness with only an isolated pinprick of light. But it's so high that no one can look in, and I get the same feeling I used to get in my chestnut tree in Summerfield.

I turn with a smile. "Maybe I was a seagull in another life. I love being up high, so this is amazing."

Anna grins. "The kitchen is behind the breakfast bar like mine. Stove, refrigerator and washing machine provided, but no dishwasher, dryer or heating. There's no gas in the building so we have electric showers and you need to buy your own room heaters. It's like the Arctic up here in the winter, Lizzie, so you'll need some big rugs to cover these old wooden floorboards as well."

My bedroom is a smaller room with the same view. It has two empty closets with the doors hanging open. Against one wall is a table and next to it, a bed frame with no mattress.

"The last tenant, Mario, left those. He's gone back to Italy now. Those should be okay once they are sanded down and painted."

Anna turns the shower on in the bathroom, and the pipes make a loud knocking sound. She turns the jet on and off several times, and the noise stops. "This is ancient plumbing, and because of how high you are, the pump struggles to get water way up here. If Harry's in the shower below you and you don't turn it off and on again like this, he'll get a blast of freezing cold water!"

We giggle, and I quickly turn my thoughts away from Harry in the shower. Anna hands me my keys, and I enjoy feeling the weight of them in my hand. "Thanks so much for showing me everything, Anna. I need to find somewhere to stay for tonight, though. Is there a bed and breakfast nearby?"

"Och, don't be silly. I've got an inflatable mattress and bed linen if you'd like to borrow them. You could make up the bed in here and find some stuff tomorrow."

"That would be great."

"I'll bring up milk and tea bags, too. And there's a Chinese take-out and a fish and chip shop just along the road." She turns toward the door. "I've just completed a big design job, so I could take you out and show you where things are tomorrow. You can get most things you'll need in the Edinburgh markets."

I treat Anna to a Chinese meal and on the way back, she points to the brown door on the second floor. "Donal lives here, but he's away until Friday. He stays with his mum and dad, keeps an eye on them when he's working on the other side of the city."

It's odd to think that my brother lived in that apartment for the three years of his university course, and now I live in The Warehouse too. I'll have to take some pictures for Dan to show him the place now. I head upstairs and make up the bedding. It's freezing in the apartment and it smells musty. I'm looking forward to transforming it into somewhere I can feel at home again.

It's not long before I'm wrapped tight in Anna's comforter with her air mattress on a frame like a hospital bed beneath me. I watch the moonlight move across the floor of the empty apartment and feel a pang of homesickness. It's quiet up here, but the noises of the city still filter up from outside, not the sounds of the dogs in the yard or the ponies in the barn. I miss everything about Home Farm. I miss the animals and my warm kitchen. I miss Clair and Mum on a good day. A rising wind from the Firth of Forth finds a crack in the fire escape door, whistles underneath, and rattles it. It puts my nerves on edge. Am I doing the right thing, moving so far away from everything I know and love?

* * *

Bright sun wakes me early, and in the morning light, the rooms look entirely different. Like an empty canvas waiting to be painted. A sense of possibility fills me, and I jump out of bed still wrapped in the comforter. Is that really ice on the window sill? Sure enough, it is. But out the window, there's a vast expanse of blue sky with big white clouds, and a sliver of the sea flashes silver between the buildings. I can now see a thousand ways to make this apartment into my new home.

Anna's up early too, so we head to the markets. We have fun finding bargains from my essentials list, and I buy a brand new mattress, a nearly new couch, and a big desk. A 'man with a van' promises to deliver that afternoon. "Donal has a business like that," Anna says. "He'd have helped us if he'd been here."

We get to know one another as we walk and shop. "How long have you lived in Edinburgh, Anna?"

"Och, all my life. I was born here. My father, Ewan MacDonald, was from Leith and in the Merchant Navy. My Jamaican grandfather, Horace, brought his whole family here in the boom years of the docks. My mum, Doreen, met Dad at a dance when they were both eighteen, but Mum was a seamstress, and the family needed her wages. She told me they were courting for five years before Granddad permitted them to marry. Back then, mixed-race marriage was not so acceptable. Mum was so lonely after Dad passed away, so she moved down to Brixton, a lively Afro-Caribbean area, to be closer to her two sisters. But she comes back here to see me a lot because she loves Edinburgh. I go to see them, but to be honest, I can only take London in small doses. My home and work are here. What about you, Lizzie? Where's your family?"

I give her a quick overview of growing up in Oxfordshire.

"Charlie, my dad is in Australia, with his second family and Dan is now married to Jenna, making a new life in Idaho, in the USA. Our mum has Alzheimer's and she's just gone into a care home."

"Oh, I'm sorry." Anna looks sympathetic as we board the bus back to Leith. "You've come a long way, but give it a wee bit of time, and you'll love Edinburgh, I know it."

Back at The Warehouse, Anna lends me an old smock, and I put on my old jeans from home. We put down drop cloths, and she helps me to decorate the walls with some leftover paint. I've chosen a soft, chalky white color and bought lengths of gauzy white fabric to soften the outline of the windows. I'm having such fun that I also paint the scruffy closets and the metal frame of my bed a deep matte black. Anna has made me buy thermal underwear, a dehumidifier, and a big heater that can be wheeled from room to room. It sits waiting at the side of the room as we paint with the windows wide open, the cold air sweeping through, taking the paint smell away. It feels like a new start.

Over the next few days, the apartment is transformed. The new coat of paint has freshened up the walls, there are big colorful Indian rugs on the floors, plus loads of gorgeous cushions and throws on my couch. I found attractive side lamps so I don't have to use the overhead strip light. Picture frames display all my family, and the dogs and ponies come to join me in my new life. I've got the hang of the heater and the shower, and now I'm warm and toasty in my new home.

That afternoon, a garden center utility van pulls up, and the guys puff up the stairs with my houseplants in big pots. Tall, spiky bamboo, flat rubber plants and feathery sage with its clean scent. I put two elegant weeping figs in matching soft blue ceramic pots next to the door to my bedroom. Anna comes up to have a look.

"Wow, this place is transformed! You've made it beautiful, Lizzie. In good time too, because the students are back tomorrow. We need to go over all the custodian stuff so you can take it over completely. I've brought the folder with me."

We sit down on the couch, the folder opened between us and go through everything I need to do.

"It won't take too long, and you can get the cleaning done in batches and keep the students in order. You'll have time to get another job too – or did you have anything else planned?"

I shake my head. "I definitely need to get a job. I've used up nearly all my savings and the money Viv sent me from the sale of the furniture at Home Farm on this place. But it's worth every penny." I look around with satisfaction at my cozy apartment. "I'd love to have a housewarming now that I have pans and ingredients for baking. Will you come up for a celebration afternoon tea tomorrow?"

"Of course, I'm honored. And I do love cake! 'Til tomorrow then."

* * *

Next morning, I do my first grand clean through The Warehouse, making it shipshape as the students arrive back for their new term. I put dried lavender in jars on the landing window sills to add soft color and help the old place smell better. Once that's all done, I start to bake. I have to get used to the oven, but it feels so good to get back into cooking again. Singing softly as I work, I finally feel like I'm settling in, and soon, the wonderful smells of baking fill the air.

I make a big tray of chocolate cupcakes, decorate them with piped icing stars, and take them down to the students. They are settling in and come to their doors, grinning as they see free food. I take the opportunity to tell them that I'm the custodian and go over the fire regulations. Munching moist chocolate cupcakes helps the medicine of expected behavior go down. They seem like a nice bunch.

While the next batch of cakes are in the oven, I lay a crisp white cloth on my table and place floral napkins on pretty plates. I place a small cut-glass vase from the thrift store filled with wild flowers in the center. After all, this needs to be a proper celebration.

As four o'clock approaches, I lay out our afternoon tea. Pride of place goes to my Victoria sponge cake, fluffy and beautifully risen, its layers sandwiched together with thick vanilla buttercream icing and raspberry jam. Next to it, a dark ginger loaf oozing with treacle and a delicate platter of plain and fruit scones with a dish of fresh clotted cream and another of Scottish plum preserves.

Just as I'm setting out the cups and saucers and about to make the tea, there's a knock on the door. I glance up at the clock. Anna's early, but that's fine. "Just a moment." I take off my apron and smooth down the front of my dress. I usually live in jeans, but I'm wearing this for our first girls' tea party. I take off my glasses and open the door with a flourish.

But it's not Anna.

It's a drop-dead gorgeous man. He's tall, around six foot two, with soft dark hair, serious green eyes, and a wide welcoming smile.

"Hello Lizzie, I'm Donal. Anna's on her way up for afternoon tea and said to come say hi to you. I could smell your baking as soon as I came in the door. Room for one more?"

Chapter 6

I'm staring up at Donal, stuttering over a welcome as Anna runs up the stairs. "Wow, that smells amazing. I'm starving."

Her words remind me of my manners, and I turn away from the handsome Scot and indicate the table. "Please come in, Donal, there's plenty, and of course, you're welcome to stay."

There's a look of delight on his face as he steps into the apartment, ducking his head a little. "Thanks. You are seriously welcome at The Warehouse. We do love a baker." He looks around, and the place feels much smaller with him in it – in a good way. "You've done amazing things with the place in such a short time."

We have a happy afternoon with tea and cake, with Anna and Donal telling stories of past Warehouse tenants good and bad. I can't help sneaking glances at him as we eat, and I can't get enough of his warm Scottish burr. He glances at his watch after sundown and heads off to another job. Anna offers to help me clear up.

As soon as Donal has gone, I turn on her, hands on my hips. "A man with a van, you said. You made him sound mundane, Anna, but he's handsome and so nice. Aren't you interested in him?"

Anna giggles as she carefully washes a bone china teacup, one of the mismatched set I managed to get on a vintage market stall. "What? Yon man? No, he's not my type for romance. I just thought you'd enjoy a wee surprise."

I look toward the door. "I certainly did."

* * *

The next day, I head to the Job Center in the City and register for catering jobs. They have a board with options on it, as well as higher education possibilities. There's a flyer for the Art College advertising a limited number of places for late-entry students. Although I try to focus on the baking jobs, I find myself completing the online application for the art course.

As I press Send, the two sides of my brain argue with each other. What are you doing? You don't stand a chance of being accepted, even if you can get the money together. But if I get an interview, someone will tell me if I have any promise, and I need that.

I sigh and go back to sifting through jobs in hospitality and catering, comparing the rates of pay, bus fares and travel times. Everything has long hours for low pay. Maybe I'll look for a little café in Leith, so I could walk to work and at least have a little time for creative work.

On my way back to The Warehouse, I check my email, and there's an invite for an interview on Friday at the Art College Open Day. A bubble of excitement expands in my stomach. Shall I call Clair? Email Harry? Go and tell Anna? No, I haven't been accepted, and even if I am, there's still the reality of fees.

Early on Friday, I quietly slip away from The Warehouse, my art portfolio tucked under one arm. The bus winds its way into the city, and I'm alternately afraid, excited, and then terrified. At the college, I edge up the big flight of wide stone steps between the groups of students chatting about art with a confidence I envy. Could I ever belong here?

The walls of the imposing building are hung with amazing art, and I linger to look before following the signs for Open Day: Pre-degree Course. It leads to a huge hall with an exhibition of last year's degree work and students showcasing recent projects. I'm fascinated and lose myself in art heaven until an administrator suddenly calls my name.

"Elizabeth Martin?" She places a check mark on her list. "Please come this way. You're in Room Four with Alex, one of our lecturers in fine arts and sculpture."

I push my glasses up on my nose and take a deep breath as the door swings open. A guy in his late 30's with a beard jumps up and comes over to shake my hand. "Welcome, Elizabeth."

"It's Lizzie, if that's okay."

"Lizzie, it is then. I'm Alex. Let's see what you've brought to show me."

I fumble with the cords of the portfolio and reveal my drawings of the mares, our stallion, and the dogs playing in the yard. Alex picks them up one by one and lays them out on the wide bench. I bite my lips as he examines them.

"I don't have any qualifications or art training." My voice is quiet.

"But that's one of the reasons you want to study with us, isn't it?" Alex holds up a sketch of Jester. "And you have an eye for animal portraits, that's for sure. Few of the world's greatest artists had any formal qualifications. Pablo Picasso produced over fifty thousand pieces of work: paintings, sculpture, ceramics, plus many thousands of drawings, prints, and tapestries. But he had no qualifications."

His words make me feel more confident, not that I could ever be Picasso, of course. "I didn't know that."

Alex thoughtfully considers another piece of work. "You

can certainly draw, Lizzie. You've captured a real sense of movement in this. What art options do you want to take?"

"I've only just arrived in Edinburgh and won't be able to study full-time. What would you suggest?"

He grabs a brochure from a pile and points out various courses as he explains. "All entry-level students rotate through classes in different media plus you pick one to specialize in. If you can't come full-time, we have evening and weekend modules that all lead to the degree. It just takes longer. Is this something you want to do?"

I nod. "More than anything in the world. I just have to find the money."

He replaces the drawings in my portfolio. "Obstacles can be overcome if you care enough. My recommendation to the Admissions Office will be to offer you a place. Good luck, and I hope to see you in one of my classes."

He hands me my portfolio, we shake hands, and I walk out with wings on my feet. A professional lecturer has just said that my work is good enough to do a degree in art at Edinburgh University.

Back at The Warehouse, I call Viv and tell her everything. She's excited for me and wants to know all the details. I tell her about the course and then get onto the topic of money. "Is there any way you could be guarantor of a student loan?"

"Send me the details, Lizzie. I'll speak with Sid and get back to you."

I try to work on a job application but pounce on my phone when Viv calls back. Then a miracle happens.

"Lizzie, the money from Home Farm is in a Trust Fund for Christine's care. But Sid and I are Trustees, and the investments he's made for her are paying all the costs. We think there's enough to pay your fees for one year full-time at college plus living expenses. We can talk about things after that."

I gasp, hardly able to contain my excitement. "Oh, that's amazing. If you're sure?"

"Of course, love. Christine paid for Dan to do four years of full-time teacher training, but you had nothing. You helped your mum a lot when she needed you, and you've lost your home and livelihood. Well done on getting a place at college, Lizzie. We know it hasn't been easy for you. Sid and I are so proud of you."

When I come off the phone, I can't help but happy dance around the apartment. I'm going to art college! Sometimes the best opportunities emerge from the darkest moments, and I am determined to make the most of this one. I'm desperate to share the good news, so I call Clair and send emails to Dan, Harry, Maggie and my dad. When I tell Anna, she's delighted for me, too.

Everything is bubbling through my mind, and I'm fizzing with energy as I complete the weekly clean of The Warehouse with a smile on my face and a song in my heart.

Today, I'm also replacing the old light bulbs with new eco-LEDs. Time for this old place to go green and sustainable. I warn everyone about the imminent power outage and turn off the main power switch under the stairs. I'm up on a stepladder with a flashlight, wrestling with the bulb by the front door when Donal comes in.

"Do you need any help with that?"

I look down at him, in the beam of the flashlight. Oh, but he is a handsome man. "That would be so kind, Donal. I haven't even managed to change one bulb yet. I keep wobbling around."

"Hang on then, I've got a better stepladder in my van."

I'm still trying to remove the bulb when he returns. I turn to climb down the ladder, wobbling a little, teetering on one edge. Just as I'm about to fall, Donal reaches up with his huge hands and swings me gently through the air and onto the floor. He keeps his hands there for a moment as we stand in the semi-darkness. My heart is pounding from almost falling and being so close to him.

"Thank you." I manage to stutter.

He grins. "Anytime." I blush as he turns and moves The Warehouse ladder to one side and nimbly climbs up a brand new aluminum stepladder. He wraps a soft cloth around the old bulb and gives it a sharp twist with the ease of someone who's done this many times before. "These old bulbs shatter easily. Could you pass me a new one, please, Lizzie?"

Together, we go around the building and replace all the bulbs. When I turn on the main power again, the new lights twinkle, reflecting off the bright green paint of the walls and stairways. "That's great, thank you so much. Everything looks so much brighter."

Donal smiles. "These eco-bulbs should last at least a year, so we'll be less likely to break our necks on the stairs. Harry should have done this months ago."

I want to defend Harry and point out that Anna was the custodian before me, but I'm grateful for Donal's help and don't want to argue. "Anna's coming up later to have an Italian dinner with me. I'm celebrating my acceptance into art college. Would you like to join us for dinner?"

He beams down at me. "That would be awesome. The only Italian food I have is take-out pizza."

"See you at eight o'clock, then."

Upstairs in my apartment, I start cooking, suddenly even more motivated than ever to make the best meal for a hungry Scot. I prepare the lasagna and then knead dough – my hand-made bread is always a winner. I need to clean my glasses several times, but at last, it's all in the oven and baking slowly. I unpack the gorgeous, sparkly mini-dress that I haven't worn since Maggie and Greg's wedding. It's great to wear it again, and I brush out my hair, swirling it around my shoulders. I add a little makeup, trying not to see this as a date, especially as Anna is coming, too.

Donal arrives on the dot of eight dressed in black jeans with a fitted white shirt that hugs his muscular torso. A wide black belt with a big buckle encloses his slim waist. He hands me a bottle of Italian red wine. "The guy in the wine store said this is *elegant, composed and a bit playful.*" He smiles. "It sounded like you, so I bought it." He bends to kiss my cheek, and I breathe in his distinctly masculine shampoo and aftershave. "You look beautiful in that dress, Lizzie."

"Thank you. The wine glasses are on the table. Would you do the honors?"

I pull the white drapes at the windows to one side so that the red candles shine double, reflected in the glass. Donal pours the wine as Anna arrives, dressed in her favorite rainbow colors and a purple shawl around her shoulders. "Lizzie, this looks simply lovely."

Donal hands Anna and me a glass of wine, his eyes sea-green in the candlelight. He smiles and raises his glass. "To Lizzie and her Italian restaurant."

Anna joins him in the toast. "And congratulations on your place at art college."

We drink together and then sit down on my upholstered but mismatched dining chairs from the local junk shop. I've also moved the table nearer to the door at the top of the fire escape so that I can look at the sky when I eat or work. I've made a stuffed sausage of a draft excluder to stop the wind that comes under the door, so it's lovely and warm now.

I unwrap the bread from a white linen cloth, and it releases the aroma of warm herbs. "This is my focaccia, an Italian flatbread with garlic, thyme, and a scattering of sea salt pressed into the top."

There are stuffed olives and sun-dried tomatoes on the table, which Anna and I nibble on as Donal digs in with gusto. I laugh at the look of pleasure on his face.

He grins. "I've never tasted home-baked Italian bread before. This is heaven." He leans back in his chair, and I realize I don't know much about him.

"I know a bit about Anna now, Donal. But how did you come to live at The Warehouse?"

He lifts his glass, the deep red liquid reflecting the candlelight. "I'm the youngest of three brothers and left school early to work for a building company in Edinburgh before I started my own handyman business. It's starting to pick up now, and I get a lot of odd jobs around this time of the year. My brothers are married with kids and they think I should live at home to support Mum and Dad, who are getting old now. But I need my own life, and I think we should all share that responsibility."

I nod sympathetically, thinking of Mum and my life at Home Farm. "I understand completely."

The oven pings and I take my padded gloves to lift a bubbling lasagna onto the table, rich with toasted cheese and a deep red tomato sauce that shows around the sides. "This is my specialty with a choice of minced beef or roasted vegetables. But leave some space, because I've also made tiramisu for dessert."

We eat the lasagna together with a crisp salad and more wine, enjoying the dessert afterward, light, cold and sweet after the warming pasta. It's a relaxed and jolly evening with interesting stories and lots of laughter. Anna picks up the empty wine bottle and looks at it with a raised eyebrow. "I'll just pop downstairs and fetch us another."

Anna leaves the door partially open, and as her footsteps fade down the stairs, Donal moves his chair closer to mine. He takes my hand. I'm mesmerized by the candlelight reflecting in his eyes, the curve of his soft mouth as he leans in, his face close to mine. I can hardly breathe.

"Lizzie, I wanted to ask you –"

There's a creak as the door swings open again.

"Hey, guys. I just met Anna and … "

Harry stands in the doorway, his words trailing off, his eyes like a stormy dark ocean as he sees us together.

Chapter 7

"Harry!" There's a surge of joy in my heart to see him. I let go of Donal's hand and jump to my feet, meeting Harry half-way across the room. "I didn't know you were coming back today."

He pulls me into a long hug, then releases me to kiss my cheek. "It's good to see you, Lizzie. I just got in. Hi, Donal."

"Harry." Donal's voice has an edge of steel in it now as he sits back in his chair, folding his arms.

Harry looks around at the apartment. "This place looks amazing. I like the new bulbs and the lavender on the window sills." I catch his glance at the table.

"Donal helped me with the light bulbs. Have you eaten? There's some lasagna left with salad and focaccia if you're hungry."

"I thought I could smell your wonderful cooking, I'd love some. I'm ravenous, and there wasn't even a bag of peanuts on the late flight from London."

He pulls out the chair on the fourth side of the table and sits down just as Anna arrives with the second bottle of wine. She's puffing. "Goodness me, that pasta makes the stairs seem a long way."

She greets Harry as I bring the leftovers out and Anna

tops up our wine glasses. Harry lifts his glass and my spirits soar to see the admiration in his eyes. "I got your email. Many congratulations on getting into art school. I knew you were good enough. Way to go!"

I blush as he catches hold of my hand and kisses the back. Then he piles his plate and hungrily, begins to eat. "Oh, this is sensational. I think you may have saved my life. I was contemplating cold baked beans from a tin."

Donal stands up suddenly. "Thanks for a great dinner, Lizzie, but I need to go. Early start tomorrow morning."

I walk to the door with him. "Donal, I –"

"Goodnight, all." He strides out without looking back, and I stand for a minute, staring after him.

"Did I interrupt something?" Harry says, and I wonder whether he did, or whether it was all in my mind.

I turn back with a smile. "No, of course not."

I sit down opposite Harry as he eats. He normally has short hair and a neatly trimmed beard, but since he's just back from some assignment in the wild, he has a red beard, and his hair is tied back with a leather cord. He looks tired, but he flashes me a crinkly-eyed smile, the tan showing off his white, even teeth. I realize again how much he means to me, and what being with him does to my pulse rate. I struggle to contain my grin as I think about what Clair would say. Two men I fancy in one house. What's a girl to do?!

"I'll tell you about the trip in a minute, but first, I want to hear everything about college, Lizzie. Sorry I could only send a one-liner when I got your email. We were heading into the mountains, and there was no reception. So, tell me everything."

Anna listens to my excitement all over again, but she doesn't seem to mind and sips her wine as I tell Harry about the Open Day, the interview and about Viv giving me the money from Mum's Trust Fund. "She says to talk to her and

Sid again at the end of Year One. Depending on how the investments perform, they may be able to help me next year as well."

Harry smiles with pleasure for me, and it's the closest I've felt to being at peace for far too long. "You so deserve this chance, Mouse. When we were kids, you loved to draw. Dan and me, we went off to college, but you couldn't. So, now is your time. Enjoy it!"

I'm all talked out, and I take off my glasses to rub my eyes and lay them on the table. Anna makes us all some peppermint tea. "Your turn Harry, tell us about Bali."

Harry leans back, relaxed and full of good food. He puts his hands behind his head, looking over at me in the candlelight. Anna brings the tea and sits down again, wrapping her hands around her mug.

"Bali must be one of the most beautiful places in the world," he says. "We did the beach shoots for swimwear, and there was time to snorkel in the warm, blue water with loads of different fish and corals. The Balinese people are gentle, mostly Hindu and vegetarian. Their food is exquisite. Fragrant curries made with spices and coconut."

Anna and I are held in the spell of Harry's voice as he continues. "The second part of the work was in the mountains near Ubud working on images for the tourist brochures. We traveled in Jeeps through volcanoes and thick jungle."

In my mind, I see the mountains and tropical jungle, the terraces for cultivating rice and vegetables, the waterfalls, and part of me wishes I could be as adventurous as Harry.

"There was one scary moment, though." Harry's voice drops and his eyes are suddenly far away. "We were in a small boat crossing a lake when a storm blew up, without any warning. Sheets of hot rain hammered down. The boat was so low in the water as we tried to bail out the flooding, and I couldn't see the shore anymore. We tried to hold plastic over the equipment but the wind became a howling gale, and we ended up huddling over the cameras." Harry turns and meets my eyes. "I thought of you being here, Lizzie, and I wanted to come home."

He's quiet for a moment and sips his tea. I want to reach out and hold him or take his hand, but Anna breaks the silence by talking about some clients Harry knows. It feels like the right moment to put my glasses back on and clear the table.

We all share the clearing away and washing up, chatting about the new students, stuff about The Warehouse, then we say goodnight, and Anna heads downstairs. On my landing, Harry holds me close in a bear hug, and I close my eyes, happy to be in his arms. He looks down into my upturned face, and for a moment, I feel our hearts beating together. "Goodnight, Lizzie. I'm so glad to see you happy and settled here. You've made this apartment into a home. It feels like you, truly warm and kind."

* * *

It's a brilliant autumn Sunday when I wake. I stretch luxuriously as the sunshine streams in and seagulls fly past my window. Their laughing cries always make me smile, as if one of them has just told a rude joke that I can't understand. I reach for my glasses, then slip on my robe and warm slippers, make a cup of tea and carry it back to bed. The Italian dinner turned out well, and it won't be the last time I entertain up here, that's for sure.

I think of Donal leaving abruptly and wonder what he was about to say. Had there been a moment between us? He did mention maybe going for a walk today. Nothing definite but it would be good to spend some time with him – without Harry interrupting. My phone pings with a text from Harry, even though he must be downstairs in bed beneath me.

Morning, Mouse. Anna, me, Nick and his girlfriend, Kate, are going surfing. Want to come?

Surfing in Scotland, whatever next? It seems totally crazy. I hold my glasses up to the light and polish the lenses. I've seen people with elastic bands holding their glasses on, but it looks awkward. Anyway, I never had the opportunity to learn to surf, and if it's this cold in Edinburgh city, it will be freezing on the coast. I snuggle deeper under the quilt. I'll stay here and maybe go for a walk and a coffee with Donal later.

But then I think of Harry and the sun sparkling on the ocean. I came to Scotland to experience a new life, not to huddle in bed. And Harry will be gone again tomorrow.

Would love to but I can't surf. I'll come and take pictures instead. See you soon.

Thirty minutes later, Harry comes bounding up the stairs to get me. His beard is gone again, he's clean-shaven, and the bottom half of his face is lighter than the rest without a tan. His hair is clean and tied back again. He looks like a buccaneer and roars with laughter as he looks me up and down. I grin at him, not caring about being decorative today. I'm in thermal leggings under baggy jeans with thick socks and hiking boots, a working man's plaid shirt, and a huge sweater with a waterproof jacket on top. I waggle my fingers in their knitted gloves, each finger a different color.

"Anna's been getting to you, Lizzie. It's not THAT cold in Edinburgh."

"Better to be warm, though." My hair tangles in the wind so I've braided it down my back. I pull on my blue beanie hat, grab my backpack, lock the door and follow Harry downstairs. Anna is waiting outside, dressed like me and we giggle together.

Harry shakes his head. "I'm not sure we'll be able to fit you two in the car, what with all the gear."

Nick and Kate arrive, and I'm introduced. Kate climbs into the back with Anna and me, then Harry angles the surfboards over our heads. It's a tight fit, and it feels funny, like being on vacation. We laugh and chat, buy food from a supermarket on the way, then wind our way through country lanes to the beach.

After we park, we grab all the gear and walk up over some sand dunes. I'm not expecting much, to be honest, and so I stop in amazement at the top of the dunes. "Harry, your mum and Greg sent me postcards from their honeymoon. This looks just like New Zealand."

Huge waves roll in, rearing up and crashing into white foam along the beach. Past the dramatic rocky headlands, the horizon is misty, and there's not a cloud in the azure sky.

Harry points to the surf. "Perfect conditions. Let's go."

We pile everything in the lee of a sand dune, and I pull off my beanie hat. "Goodness, a fresh breeze instead of a freezing gale."

I try not to watch Harry as they all change into wetsuits.

"Could you pull the back zipper up for me, Lizzie? I can't reach."

A ripple runs through me as I touch Harry's warm skin and zip him into the wetsuit. When they're all ready, he takes a camera from his backpack, unscrews the lens cap and hands it to me.

"Why don't you use this for your pictures? It will be better than your phone, and I'd love to get some images of us surfing."

I take it from him, the weight of it heavy in my hands. Then they're off, running down the beach to the waves, carrying their surfboards, excited by the challenge of the ocean. I feel like an old aunt left to guard the valuables.

Harry is an experienced surfer and joins a group of

people further out. Kate and Nick are intermediate level and Anna is a beginner. She's laughing with some other newbies in the shallow waves, trying hard but falling off her board a lot. Having a wetsuit is essential as the water must be very cold, and the wind chill makes it feel even colder. But it looks like she's having a good time. I raise the camera and watch the action out on the water through the powerful lens of Harry's camera. I wish I could be out there, too.

My glasses are soon opaque with the salt blowing off the ocean. With a sigh, I clean them again and decide to make the most of what I have. I look at silhouettes and take photos with the ocean fractured into splinters of light behind them. I capture Anna upright on her surfboard, knees bent into a perfect position before she tumbles headfirst into the water again. I shoot sunlight through dune grasses and dogs playing chase. The Scottish cold and rain are forgotten as I strip off layers of clothing, then I sit against a dune with my sketch pad, drawing rapid impressions of the scene before me. It's a beautiful day, but I'd rather be out there with my friends than stuck on the beach.

Anna tires first and comes slowly back up the beach. She drops her surfboard and drinks a whole bottle of water. I show her my photos, and she grins at the one of her on the surf board. "Oh, that's awesome. I look like I know what I'm doing. My family won't believe it." She strikes a surfer pose. "Look, I can really surf!"

Then the others come back, and Nick sets up the mini barbecue. We grill chicken satay skewers and halloumi cheese, sitting in the sun to eat them with salad and pita bread with grapes for dessert.

After lunch, Harry sits higher up the dune with his camera and looks at the shots I've taken. He's still in his wetsuit, but the top part is peeled to his waist and hangs down. He wears a faded denim shirt, buttoned, but with the sleeves rolled up. I take off my glasses and lie on one side, loving the caress of the sun on my closed eyelids.

"You look beautiful just there, Lizzie." Harry's voice is soft. "The sun is so bright on your hair. Sit up, I'll take some more shots."

Anna leans over and unties my braid. I sit up and let my hair blow in the breeze, running my fingers through it and shaking it out. Harry takes rapid photographs, and I feel like one of his models caught in the sunshine.

"Turn this way, now drop your head back. Yes, that's good. Lean forward a little, so your hair hides your face. Now, look up at me."

I suddenly feel self-conscious. "Okay, that's enough. Stop now, please Harry." I reach for my glasses, but he catches my hand.

"Just a couple more. Your hair looks just like the ripples in the shallow water."

I can't help but smile because he makes me feel beautiful. He pulls away, and I put on my glasses again, feeling like I'm putting a barrier up between us. "I'll edit these, and send you the best."

Nick picks up his board. "Time for a few more runs?"

I gather my hair into a scrunchy and wave them off. "You guys go. I'll clear the barbecue and pack up."

They grab the surfboards, but Anna decides she's had enough for one day and stays to help. She points to a group having a lesson. "We'll get you a wetsuit next time."

But I want to shout in frustration. It's not the wetsuit; it's my glasses.

On the journey home, Harry jumps into the back seat between Anna and me as Kate drives. We no longer have our big coats on and he laughs, putting one arm around each of us. "Hey, this is a neat sandwich with me in the middle." I snuggle under his arm, happy after such a great day out.

Back at The Warehouse, we say goodnight to Nick and

Kate then rinse all the surfing gear under the outside tap. Anna goes to bed and Harry and I wearily climb the last stone stairs. At his door, Harry hugs me. "I'm so glad you came. Did you have fun?"

"It was wonderful. Thanks for inviting me. I only wish I could surf."

"Maybe next time. I'm off early tomorrow for two weeks, working in Spain. I'll see you when I get back."

I climb the last flight of stairs warmed by the memories of the day. It felt different with Harry today, and I want more. As I walk into the apartment, I feel a chill breeze from the outside, then the door to the fire escape rattles in the rising wind. It will only get worse as the winter draws in. Before I forget, I grab my phone and send Harry a quick text.

> *Great fun today, thank you again. Could you please order a deadbolt for my fire escape door? It's not secure, and Donal says it must be fitted by a locksmith for your insurance. Lx*

A moment later, a text comes back.

> *On my list. Hx*

Next morning, Harry heads to the airport early, and I hear the taxi pulling away as I lie in bed. I think of him, so confident in the ocean and when he meets new people. I want that kind of confidence as I head to a new life in art school.

And I really want to surf next time.

An idea begins to surface again, one I had pushed down as just vanity at the time, but now it might just be the right time before I start at art school in earnest. Before Mum was diagnosed, I secretly went for an assessment at a clinic in Oxford, but I chickened out and didn't go through with it.

Before I can change my mind, I phone the clinic.

"Yes, Miss Martin, your details are still on our system. We have a cancellation for this evening. Would you like the appointment?"

I manage to book a domestic flight online and catch Clair before she starts teaching her first class. "Tell you everything when I see you, but could you pick me up in Oxford this evening? And can I stay for a couple of days?"

"Of course, Lizzie, I'm intrigued. Call me when you're ready."

I pack quickly and head downstairs with my bag, stopping in at Anna's on the way down.

"Och, it's cold out here," she says. "What's up?"

"I need to go away until Thursday night. Could you cover for me as custodian?"

"Of course." She yawns. "Are you okay? What are you up to?"

I take a deep breath. "Yesterday was the last straw with my glasses. I'm going to have laser surgery and get rid of them forever."

Chapter 8

Later that day, I'm standing alone and terrified outside an Oxford eye clinic. Am I really going to let someone do laser surgery on my eyes? What if I go blind? Is this just a crazy idea? I'm about to turn and run when a man comes out of the building and holds the door for me. "Going in?"

I take a deep breath. "Yes, thank you."

Inside, the clinic is calm with pictures on the walls of happy people doing exciting things. One woman is even surfing, a wide smile on her face. It makes me determined to go on, so I sign the consent forms and the surgeon comes in. I'm glad to see that it's the same woman I saw for my assessment. "Hi, Lizzie, I've got all your notes, and we're good to go. Come on through."

A nurse gives me a gown to change into, and my heart thunders in my chest as she helps me onto the padded table. I lie on my back and stare up into bright lights and shiny machinery. On one side, the surgeon looks down into the microscope. "Breathe deeply and relax, Lizzie. There's no need to worry. Today's technology means we'll correct one eye and then do the other, right after. You'll be out of here in no time at all."

She continues to talk quietly, looking at my right eye.

The little girl inside me is glad to have a kind nurse holding my hand. I follow all the instructions, and it feels strange as the procedure happens quickly: unpleasant, but not particularly painful. I breathe steadily, thinking of Harry and surfing in the waves next to him, his arms around me, pulling off his denim shirt as he –

"All done." The surgeon's voice is brisk now. "Everything looks good."

"Wow, that was quick."

The nurse moves the equipment to one side and helps me sit up as the surgeon checks my eyes. "You can expect some blurring, but your vision will be up to 80% almost immediately, improving to 100% within a day or so."

"Thank you so much, that was much easier than I expected it to be."

The surgeon smiles. "Pretty much everyone says that. Have fun now."

The nurse puts some drops into my eyes, and I go out to the recovery area. I sit looking around without my glasses on, and I can already see better than I used to. My nose feels strange without the glasses on them, and I feel for the case in my bag, a habit I've had for years since losing them when I was young. I won't need to do that anymore.

I have a cup of tea, and it's not long before Clair comes to get me. We head to the car, my hand on her arm, just to steady myself a little.

"You didn't say a word about doing this. I'd have come with you, you know."

"It was a sudden decision."

"Did you do it for Harry?"

"When I first came, it was about trying to be prettier somehow, but now, it's more about wanting a new kind of confident life. I need to stop hiding, Clair. I need to stop being a mouse."

She nods. "I understand. I'm thinking about a lot of

things right now too. Granddad had a fall recently, and I suddenly realized how frail he is."

We arrive at the Stables, and I take her arm along the path to the cottage. "It's like the ground is coming up to meet me."

I hold onto the furniture in the family room as I go to sit down on the couch. I've been here so many times before but never noticed that it's like being in a cheerful country picture. A big, orange patterned rug covers the stone-tiled floor, and the cushions are embroidered with Grandma May's hand-embroidery. Her brass pans gleam and glint on the shelf in the kitchen. "Clair, this is so strange, but completely amazing."

She smiles. "I was worried when you said you were at the clinic. It's so unlike you to do something like this, but I'm pleased you're happy. I never saw your glasses anyway, to be honest, just you. But if it helps to remove that barrier, I get it." She looks at her watch. "I need to help Granddad and Robert finish up in the yard, but I'll see you in a little while."

In the guest bedroom upstairs, I text Anna to tell her that all went well. Then I stare at myself in the mirror and examine every tiny detail of my face without my glasses. Clair and I used to have teenage sleepovers in this room, so I've seen this face at many stages of life. It feels like a new start to be here again.

Later on, I hear Ted and Clair come in from the yard and go down to join them, holding tightly to the stair rail. I give Ted a hug, and we all sit down with cups of tea. "I haven't told Viv and Sid about my eyes yet. They have enough to worry about with Mum. I'll call and tell them soon, and I'm staying with them over Christmas. I just need a quiet couple of days to let my eyes adjust, but I could cook for you guys while I'm here. Is there something special you'd like?"

Ted is a fit eighty-something, gnarled like an old tree, but he looks smaller now. I know he misses May, his friend, and wife of sixty years, very much. "Could you make some of the dinners May used to make for me, Lizzie? Clair's so busy with the new program."

"I'm sorry, Granddad. Lizzie knows that I'm not a good cook." Clair shoots me a look of guilt and apology. "I alternate between baked potatoes and stir-fry, which is what we're having tonight."

"I'm not criticizing, Clair, dear. But if Lizzie is offering, I'd love a steak and kidney pudding. May used to cook it the old-fashioned way, and you couldn't beat it for taste."

I nod. "I remember my Grandma cooking what she called a meat pudding. Dan hated it, but I loved it. She'd line a big white pudding basin with suet crust then fill it with chunks of steak and kidney. She'd add lots of sliced onions and carrots and then fill the basin with a good, thick gravy."

Ted's face lights up with memory. "Suet crust on the top with an upside down saucer to keep it in place, then all tied into a white cloth with a bow on the top."

I smile and continue on from him. "Slow steamed for three hours then served straight from the basin to the plates on the table with creamy mashed potatoes, cauliflower, and tiny green peas. I'll do my best, Ted. Treacle tart and custard for dessert?"

Ted licks his lips. "Oh, come and stay with us anytime, Lizzie."

He goes off to change out of his work clothes, and I help Clair by carefully setting the table while she makes a chicken stir-fry.

"I suggested we find a cook-housekeeper," she whispers, "but Granddad won't have anyone else in this kitchen but family." Her eyes mist with tears. "I've always been cynical about marriage since Mum and Dad divorced. But I hope, one day, I might find a love like my grandparents had. They were partners all their lives and they sure laughed a lot."

I think of Harry and his wandering life. "I don't know if that kind of marriage is even possible these days."

* * *

When I wake the next morning and open my eyes, I'm struck by the intricate patterns in the old wood beams above my bed. Before the laser surgery, I'd have only seen a dark blur without my glasses. Out of the window, I can see fields with horses grazing and the beech trees in Potlatch Wood are covered with gold-coin leaves. From below, I hear the sounds of the busy stable yard with people and the clip-clop of ponies on the cobbles. I go to the window and look down to see Russ, Ted's old horse, watching everything over the door of his stall. I can't help the grin on my face. It's all so new and clear.

After breakfast, I go out with Ted to May's old chicken house. High walls separate the kitchen garden from the stables, and as it's sheltered from the wind, many of the bushes are still in flower. There are even some late bees buzzing around, and I watch them settle briefly on the petals and fly off again. The hens scratch and cluck in their run. We scatter grain for them and collect a few speckled eggs.

Ted takes my hand, and I feel the slight shaking in his once-strong grip. "Do you miss your old home, Lizzie? It must be hard to be so close and not be able to go back."

I nod. "Sometimes, but my family and our animals are gone, so it's not home anymore. I've found some friends in Edinburgh, and I'm starting a new art course next week, so I'm keeping busy." As I tell him about it all, I realize how far I've come in such a short time. I guess I just needed to get out of Summerfield to see the world differently.

I head back into the kitchen to start cooking, and I rapidly discover it's a whole new cooking experience. There is no weight resting on the bridge of my nose that slips and needs to be pushed back up with sticky hands. No foggy vision when I open the oven door. It's a revelation. I'm soon elbow deep in mixing bowls with pans simmering on the stove and bread in the oven. I make a hearty soup for lunch, a big quiche, a treacle tart and Ted's steak and kidney pudding.

The day passes quickly, and horse shoes soon clip-clop on the cobbles outside as the last riders return, and I set the table for dinner.

"Hi honey, I'm home!" Clair comes in laughing and gives both Ted and I a hug. "That smells divine."

Ted eats slowly, savoring every mouthful and I watch his face like a contestant chef on a TV show. He nods and smiles over the steak and kidney pudding. "May would have been happy with that."

I grin, delighted to give him a moment of pleasure and Clair smiles over at me, so happy that her granddad is pleased. She digs in, the rich steak gravy spilling over creamy mashed potatoes and fresh green peas. "This is amazing, Lizzie."

"I'm so glad that you like it, but I haven't had a chance to ask you, how's your Riding with Challenges Program going?"

"We have a new volunteer, Patricia Anderson, a friend of Viv's. She recently retired from school administration and moved to the village. She's marvelous. The program has started well, and we have twelve students."

I serve up the treacle tart with a jug of creamy vanilla custard, and Ted looks like a little kid as he picks up his dessert spoon.

"A large helping, please, dear. And please don't go back to Scotland!"

"Don't worry, Ted, I'll be back again to see you at Christmas, and I promise to bake again."

I spend two more days at Summerfield Stables and have the time to get into my art in preparation for the start of the course. Clair and Ted head out each morning to work with the horses, and I stay in my room away from the dust as my eyes adjust and heal. I watch the horses out the window and sketch them with a new-found focus.

Seeing the different kinds of art displayed at the college renewed my interest in other mediums and I begin to imagine a sculpture of our champion Welsh Mountain stallion, now on a stud farm in Wales. He was our best foal and a top prize winner at the prestigious Ascot Stallion Show. I looked after him, and although Mum took him into the ring, he was mine as well as hers, and I loved him.

I have sketches of him as a foal, a dear palomino baby with a white mane and tail, a yearling, and as a two- year-old. With his expressive face and beautiful conformation, he deserved the Championship. Could I make a sculpture that would do him justice? Might I do that for other owners as a business? It's a wonderful thought to consider, and it fires my enthusiasm.

I research horse sculptures online, looking at Chinese war horses from centuries ago in terracotta, fired clay, bronze and polished copper. There's a spectacular thirty-foot-high horse's head standing on its nose near Hyde Park in London, and so many other examples. I consider for the first time how much art is worth creating. After all, the food I make pleases people for a moment before it's consumed and gone. Art endures, and I want to show the magnificence of the horses I love and the unique bond that humans all over the world have with them. I spend my time sketching horses' heads in charcoal and soft black pencil, and horses lying down and scratching each other's necks.

My eyes get stronger, and I let my passion overwhelm me. I'm excited about finally moving forward. Going back to Edinburgh without glasses, I can focus on my art. It feels like a new start, and who knows, maybe even love might come along this time?

Chapter 9

On the way back from Oxford to The Warehouse, I write a list of everything I need to turn my bedroom into a sculpture studio. Now I have my ideas, I'll be learning the techniques at college, and I'm going to start work on the head of the stallion in clay, and that needs a cold environment. My bedroom is certainly that!

I traipse up the stairs, listening at Harry's door just in case, but he's not back. Anna and Donal are out, so I text them to come up for tea when they get in. I feel like celebrating. I've worn glasses since I was eleven and now I don't need to wear them anymore. Definitely something to share with friends.

I drag my bed into the living room then whip up a batch of cheese scones and pop them into the oven. I pin up the new sketches from the Stables and when the kitchen timer pings, I dash back into the kitchen to lay the scones out on a wire rack to cool.

This multi-tasking thing is fun, and I don't once miss my glasses at all because I can go so much faster without them. What's next on the list? Oh yes, drag the dining table into the sculpture room. I'll need to buy a small metal trash can with a lid to keep the clay damp. A tripod and turntable would be useful too. I'm distracted as I walk back into my living room.

The front door bangs open suddenly. I must not have shut it properly.

A big woman with snarled turquoise dreadlocks and black mascara eyes stands in the doorway. A thin chain hangs between studs in her nose and ear. She wears a black leather jacket with a short tartan skirt, and black leggings with slits across the knees. She lunges forward, pushing her bulk into the room.

"What you doin' in ma place?" Her Scottish accent is strong, and she smells of cigarettes and alcohol.

"Sorry, are you with one of the students?" I try not to sound as scared as I feel. "This is my apartment."

She walks right up to me, standing so close that I have to take a step back. "Harry said I could have this place when it was empty. So, get your wee bits together and get out of here."

"Harry's away on a work trip. You'll need to sort it out with him. But this is my apartment, and I'm the custodian of The Warehouse now."

She narrows her eyes and then turns toward the breakfast bar, sniffing the air. She saunters over, takes one of my scones and stuffs it whole into her mouth. She watches me as she chews slowly, then swallows. I don't move, listening for any sound of Donal or Anna below, or even one of the students.

"Harry promised me this place. I'll be back on Sunday with ma brother. If you're still here, then we'll help you move your stuff … out the window."

She laughs nastily as she takes two more scones and stows them in the pockets of her jacket. Then she clenches a meaty fist and grins as she enjoys smashing all the other scones to crumbs. "Sunday." She stomps out, and her boots clatter on the stairs.

I sit down abruptly, letting out the breath I'd been holding as her fist beat my scones. But then, I hear her feet running back up again. I grab the vegetable knife from the draining board.

Anna sticks her head around the door. "What's going on? I just saw Bea leaving with a face like thunder."

I'm confused. "Bea? I thought Bea was one of Harry's girlfriends!"

Anna gently takes the knife from my hand. "No, Bea was a friend of ours in our first year at university. Harry took a lot of pictures of her and her band in the early days before they got into hard drugs. He visited her in rehab a couple of times, but he hasn't mentioned her in a while. I heard she might have been in prison."

I lean against the breakfast bar, my legs still weak from the shock. "She said that Harry promised her this apartment."

Anna frowns. "Well, some of the things Bea says are true, but she also makes up a lot of stuff. I know, as the former custodian, that Harry would not have offered her an apartment without telling me first."

"But she says I'm to be gone by Sunday and Harry won't be back by then. What am I going to do?"

"We'll think of something, but let's go and ask Donal. I just heard his van, and he's always got good ideas for practical difficulties." Anna pauses to look at me more closely. "I just noticed the glasses are gone. How does it feel?"

"As if the real me can emerge, but I wanted to tell you and Donal all about it over tea." I point to the countertop at the crushed scones. "But Bea's ruined that. What was she in prison for?"

"Assault, and grievous bodily harm."

"Oh, great, just what I need."

I head downstairs to find Donal. He welcomes me inside his typical bachelor pad with washing drying on a rack, a sports bag next to the enormous TV, and a faint smell of socks. Donal listens as I re-tell what happened.

"She must have slipped in behind one of the students. The spring means that door closes quite slowly. You'll need to keep your inside door locked from now on. I'll hook up a CCTV camera on your landing, so we'll have evidence for the police if she comes again."

I'm grateful for his practical help. "Thanks, that makes me feel better. I made cheese scones. Bea mangled them all, but I'm going up to make some more right now. Come up for a fresh batch in about forty minutes?"

Later, after tea, Donal lingers when Anna goes back downstairs. "Now you're back, Lizzie, would you like to see some of the sights of Edinburgh with me this Sunday? It would take your mind off Bea, and you won't be here in case she comes back."

I remember the night of the Italian dinner. Maybe he was about to ask me out. "I'd love to." As he walks out the door, he turns. "Just so you know, Lizzie, you look great without your glasses. But then I thought you looked great *with* them."

* * *

The following week is a whirlwind as I settle into the routine at college. After getting lost on the first day, I soon find a group of friends in the other mature students on the course. We do our various classes and join up for lunch every day to compare assignments. I love walking into class every day, clutching my portfolio and just doing art. It feels like this is where I'm meant to be. Alex, who interviewed me, turns out to be my tutor and he helps me with the ideas for the horse's head sculpture. Every day, I'm learning more and later that week, I buy the clay and a container to store it in at home, ready to start my new project.

On Sunday, I meet Donal down by his van. It has *Man with a Van: Full removals and single items, garden clearance, eBay collection and much more* on the side. He stands proudly by the side and holds the door open.

"Your business must be doing well, if you only have Sundays off," I say as he drives out from The Warehouse parking lot and turns onto the main road.

"One of the mixed blessings of working for myself is that I can never say no to a job."

I look at his large, capable hands on the steering wheel, remembering them around my waist that day on the stepladder. "Then thank you for sharing your precious rest day with me."

"My pleasure, especially after the fabulous food you've been cooking. The way to this man's heart is definitely through his stomach."

I don't dare mention that my dining table has moved on to become a base for my sculpture as art becomes my primary focus instead of cooking. I don't even know if I'll be having any more dinner parties, so I change the subject as I look out the window at the Edinburgh cityscape. "I've never seen so many chimney pots on houses, not even in London."

"All the cooking and heating were done with coal in the nineteenth century. Edinburgh was once called Auld Reekie, you know, because it had such terrible fog and fumes."

Donal parks the van in a side street, and as we walk, he takes my hand gently. His big hand fully encloses mine, and it feels natural and comforting, so I leave it there as we walk. "I love these cobbled back streets. We used to have cobbles like this in our barn. Look, you can see where the horses were stabled down here."

"Aye. I'd have been called Man with a Horse and Cart back then." Donal laughs.

I point upwards. "The tenements are so high and so tightly packed together here. Do you know why?"

"Back in the day, when the English attacked the city, people needed to stay inside the city walls, so they had to build upwards. These are the original high-rise apartments. Think of the servants carrying coal and water up all those stairs."

I frown. "The Warehouse is bad enough, so I hate to think of it. I'm descended from working folk, and that would have been me doing the carrying."

"But better to have physical work. I couldn't for the life of me work indoors all the time." Donal leads me through the quaint streets. "But Edinburgh has its dark history, too."

He takes me down tunnels where the poor lived in the past, and some still do. We end up looking at the death masks of Burke and Hare, Edinburgh's famous grave robbers. "They couldn't get enough bodies to sell for dissection, so they turned to murder."

I shudder. Interesting, but wasn't this supposed to be a romantic date?

We climb all the way up to Edinburgh Castle, and the view is magnificent, but Donal raves on about Scotland's military history and I'm getting tired, so we go for lunch. Then, I see a sign for an art exhibition. "How about we look at some paintings?"

Donal grimaces. "Not my thing, Lizzie. I'll sit here while you go look."

I sigh as I walk around the gallery alone. Harry would have been interested but he still only sees me as a little sister. I want to give Donal a chance, even though we're so different. Then I remember that he likes to do practical things, so I head back to him.

"Donal, could you help me with something?" He looks up, interested now when I sit down opposite him again. "I've started a clay sculpture for college, but it's difficult to work on my table. We have tripods in college with turntables on the top so that we can work from different angles. Do you know anywhere that might have something like that?"

Donal jumps up, full of renewed energy. "There's a guy I know who runs a scrap metal yard. I bet he'd know where to get one." We hurry back to the van. "I won't be free for another week, Lizzie, so we need to get there before he closes. Can you go no faster? D'you want I should carry you?"

I jog along beside him to avoid the indignity of a fireman's lift over his shoulder or whatever else he has in mind, but I can't help smiling at his enthusiasm now that we're away from the gallery.

On the road again, Donal focuses on driving, and I think about my sculpture. Alex is an excellent tutor, and I'm loving working with clay. I've roughed out the shape of the stallion's head, but a turntable would help in doing the detailed work. At the scrap yard, Donal dashes into the office and comes out waving a bunch of keys. "Shed 3."

We go hunting, and when I spot a metal tripod under a pile of other stuff, he pulls it out easily, his muscles clearly defined in his tight black t-shirt. "Now we need a turntable. Like a potter's wheel, right?"

It's beginning to get dark, but after some more hunting, Donal finds one. "Right, there's a welding kit next to the office. I'll quickly put these together for you. Have you got twenty pounds? I'll negotiate a good price." He slides open the door to the van and turns on the heater. "You stay here in the warm, Lizzie."

Soon after, he loads the welded unit into the back of the van and hands me four pounds change.

"That's a bargain, thank you."

After we get back, Donal carries my prize all the way up the stairs. "You are such a friend, Donal. This is just perfect." I left my bag in the van since we needed all our hands to balance the legs of the tripod as he carried the heavy end with the turntable. I slip my arm through his as we go back downstairs. "I'm really excited. I can transfer the clay head onto the turntable and start on the next stage now."

Back at the van, Donal dusts off my bag. When I take the strap, he keeps hold of it too and gently draws me into his arms. I smile up at him.

"Thank you. You've been a great help, and I've had a wonderful day out."

He bends to kiss me, and I close my eyes as I kiss him back. I like the feeling of being held close in his strong arms, I enjoy the warmth of his mouth on mine and the masculine smell of his skin.

But there's no zap of electricity, like when I'm around Harry.

As he pulls away and I open my eyes, I catch a twitch of movement at Harry's window. Is he back? Did he see Donal kissing me?

Chapter 10

Anna opens her door and grins cheekily as we pass. "Did you guys have a nice day?"

"Lovely." I turn to Donal. "I enjoyed it very much."

He smiles gently. "I enjoyed it too, Lizzie." He kisses my cheek and goes back to his apartment.

Anna beckons me over, and I give her a nudge in the ribs.

"You are such a tease."

She laughs. "You need teasing, Lizzie. You're way too serious about everything. I wanted to tell you that Bea didn't show, but Harry's back. I need to do some work now, so you can tell him what's been going on."

So Harry is here, and part of me wants to run to him, and the other wants to avoid the moment where we might have to talk about what he saw. I'm so confused, so I just nod and go up to my apartment. After a few minutes, there's a gentle tap at my door.

"Lizzie, it's me."

My heart thumps at the sound of Harry's voice. "Just a minute."

I'm tired now, so I pinch color into my cheeks before I open the door. Harry's face is tanned and his hair cut into a cool, celebrity style. He looks quite the urban professional, not like the wild man from his last trip. He gives me a quick hug and is obviously pretending he did not see me with Donal. So I pretend as well. "Your hair's short again. I like it like that. Tea?"

"Love some." He sits up at my kitchen counter as I boil the kettle. "We have stylists for the models on the shoot, and I asked one to cut it for me." He stares at me then, his eyes slightly narrowed. "There's something different about you too, Lizzie."

I bustle about finding mugs and taking the milk from the fridge. Will he get it?

"I know! It's your glasses. I can see your eyes better. Did you get contact lenses?"

I shake my head. "After that day at the beach, I was so frustrated at not being able to go with you guys or learn to surf, so I decided to have laser eye surgery. I've been thinking about it for some time, and that was the final straw."

"How was it? Are you okay?" Harry jumps up and comes around the bench. He puts a hand out to gently touch my cheek and peers intently into my eyes. For a split second, he's just a concerned friend.

But then there's a jolt of electricity. We're only a breath apart. All he needs to do is lean closer.

He hurriedly steps away. "Did it hurt?"

He returns to his seat, and I finish making the tea. "I was terrified, but it was so quick and just uncomfortable, rather than painful. My eyesight is now one hundred percent perfect. So make sure you invite me again next time you go surfing."

"Of course. That's amazing." Harry shakes his head, looking over at me with the safe width of the counter between us. "You never would have done that in the past, Lizzie. It's like you're starting to find yourself and your place here in Edinburgh." He pauses. "And you're making new friends, too. Good friends, perhaps?"

I don't reply but instead, take a sip of my tea to hide my smile. Was there just a tinge of jealousy in his tone? I like it that Harry Stewart cares who I kiss.

"We're shooting images for an equestrian catalog tomorrow," he says. "Would you like to come? They're bringing in horses and models to a stable yard we found. But it's also a rather special house that I'd like you to see. Might you be free? I'd appreciate your perspective on it."

"Sounds intriguing, but I'm at college tomorrow morning."

"You'll miss the shoot then, but could we get together when you finish class? I'm going to Costa Rica the day after and will be away for three weeks this time." He grins happily. "It's a beautiful country, and we'll have some time between locations to go surfing."

I lean forward on the bench. "Don't you ever get tired of all the traveling, Harry? Do you ever just want to be at home?"

Harry shrugs. "The Warehouse has never been home for me. It's a crash pad. I've been saving for a couple of years now with the idea of buying a place for my own photography studio." He looks around at my apartment. "Although this place has been more like home here since you came. You brought a breath of fresh air from Summerfield." He reaches for my sketchpad at the far end of the countertop. "How's the artwork coming along?"

I jump up and beckon to him excitedly. "Come and look." I throw open the doors to the bedroom. "Ta-da!"

Harry follows me, a look of surprise on his face. "You've set up a studio in here. What a brilliant idea."

I point at my wrapped sculpture on the table by the window. It's covered with a damp hessian cloth and a big plastic bag over the top. "The clay has to stay damp and not dry out too fast."

Harry looks around. "It's just the right temperature in

here for clay. But you need a couple of spotlights. I've got some small ones you can have. Hang on." Harry runs down to his apartment while I carefully move the head of the stallion, still securely wrapped, onto the turntable that Donal helped find. Harry attaches a spotlight to the window bar, plugs it in and switches it on. It immediately brightens the area, and I can see how it will be easier to work.

"One more, from the other direction." He sets it up and the angle of the second light adds even more depth, illuminating the new sketches from Summerfield on the wall. Harry walks to the walls and studies them.

"I did those when I was staying with Clair and Ted. I'm modeling the head of our stallion from Home Farm."

"May I see it?"

I hesitate. "It's not ready ..." But this is Harry, who has seen my childish sketches from a young age, and I want to know what he thinks. So I carefully unwrap the coverings. "You're the first to see it."

Under the new spotlights, I can see mistakes everywhere and itch to put on my smock and start work. Harry studies the emerging sculpture from all sides and smiles at me. "Obviously, you have lots more work to do, but look how you've captured that look over his shoulder. He's almost alive. It's a fantastic start."

I'm delighted and blush a bit at his praise. Then I carefully re-wrap the head. It's too late to work on it now. I'll start again tomorrow night. Harry yawns. "Okay, so you'll come tomorrow after college? We could meet at the Museum and then walk together. I'll text the details."

As I close down the studio, the wind smacks the fire escape door, and it rattles. My fault. I've been so busy, I haven't bothered Harry again about having the deadbolt lock installed, and I didn't tell him about Bea. Never mind. He's only here for a short time, and she didn't come today, so maybe she won't come again. I need to look after myself and not ask Harry to rescue me all the time. I wedge a lump of clay under the door and the rattling stops. Oh my, but it's cold in here. My feet and legs are like lumps of ice as I hurry to bed, reveling in my electric blanket.

* * *

When we meet outside the National Museum of Scotland the next day, Harry kisses my cheek in welcome, his eyes bright with enthusiasm. We walk through the entrance in the undercroft, and he leaps up the stairs ahead of me. I climb more slowly, gazing upwards as the stairwell opens into a huge atrium. Tiers of white iron balconies rise to a dome of sparkling glass high above.

"Oh, Harry, it's magnificent."

He stands on the white marble floor looking up at it too. "It used to be so dark and closed in, but they did a superb renovation. Now it's airy, and the light is fabulous. I've done some beautiful wedding photographs here." We climb to the top floor, looking in at each level. Harry grins at me. "So, would you like to look at Scottish History first, or the animals?"

We say it together. "Animals."

I laugh. "You know me too well!" We set off into the Natural History section, then a slow and happy wander through World Cultures, pointing out beautiful costumes and pottery to each other.

Harry links his arm through mine as we walk and talk. "This is one of my favorite places."

"In Edinburgh?"

"In the world."

I'm surprised at his words because he travels so much and yet, it's here he feels most at home. Neither of us are that interested in murderers, war, and weaponry. But as we look together at art and the natural world, it's like the click of two magnets coming together.

"I could spend hours here with all the interesting exhibits. I'll come back again soon – with my sketchbook next time."

We share a late lunch of soup and sandwiches, then emerge into the soft winter afternoon. The wind has dropped, and it's cold but not chill. We walk together along the Water of Leith under willow trees. A heron stands motionless, watching the shallow water. It's peaceful, and we're quiet together, enjoying the silence as we walk.

We pass several streets that end at the river path, then Harry stops at a long row of terraced, Victorian houses. "This is Huntly Terrace where we were shooting this morning."

We turn to walk down it away from the water. "How did it go?"

"Good. The two horses and grooms came by trailer and behaved perfectly. The models were a pain." He grimaces. "But I'm used to that."

He stops outside Number 81, one of only two detached properties in the street. It has an imposing Victorian gateway and a wide driveway along the left side. It rises three stories above us and is really rather grand, even if run down and neglected. A big wisteria vine, probably several hundred years old, twists up and over the porch. Its leaves are a pale green cascade, and it looks quiet, like it's sleeping in the cold.

Harry leads me through the gates along the front path and up the wide front steps. "It was originally built for a merchant who imported through the Leith docks. But it's been empty for a long while. Various developers submitted planning applications for student accommodation, but they were refused. It's a listed historical building, and the Council has specified certain conditions about its restoration."

I stand on tiptoe to peer through the dusty window. "I can't see much in there, but I like the stained glass above the front door."

"Come and look around the back." Harry leads me to the back of the house through an overgrown walled yard and out through a garden door into a huge, cobbled yard. It has rusty Victorian gas lamps, five stables, all closed and padlocked and a hay loft over them.

I turn around and take it all in. "It's stunning. I love the stables and you know I love cobbles anywhere. But it's going to need a lot of renovation. Could you manage that?"

His face is determined. "If I could pull together enough money to buy it, would you come and look at it again? You've got a real eye for interiors."

His words make me wonder whether my place at The Warehouse is certain, especially if Harry decides to move on. But if he committed to renovating a place, I guess he'd have to be in Edinburgh more often. I nod. "Of course, I'd love to help, and you should ask Anna, too. She has great ideas and a huge network of contacts in Edinburgh."

It's dark as we head back, with Harry talking non-stop about his ideas for the place. It's clear he's been thinking about it seriously. We end up sitting on my couch with mugs of hot chocolate discussing how Huntly Terrace might be split into studios.

As we're sitting there, I think I can hear noises out on the wasteland.

"What's that?" My heart thumps as I consider Bea might out there. I still haven't told Harry about what happened with Bea, and now it feels like I'm making too much of nothing to mention it. I get up and go to the window, looking out into the dark. Harry comes over to join me, and we stare out at the thick undergrowth lit by the lamp on the river path.

Nothing moves. There are only big elderberry bushes straggling across the smashed concrete.

"Maybe it was the wind off the estuary?" He carries our cups to the sink and rinses them then returns to hug me. "Thanks for coming today."

I put my arms around his waist and rest my head on his chest. Doesn't he feel what I feel? I want to stay here forever, safe in his arms, but he kisses my hair and then, reluctantly, I think, pulls away. I don't want him to go, but he's heading out of the door, turning just before he closes it.

"I have to leave early tomorrow. Maybe we could do something else together when I'm back again?"

"I'd like that."

I lock my door and put on the security chain. Harry clearly means to move out at some point, so would I want to stay here without him? I'm just starting to get settled here and once again, I feel the earth shift under me as the situation changes. I turn off the lights and go back to the window. I watch for ten minutes, and nothing stirs on the waste ground, but my intuition keeps nagging at me.

Someone is out there.

Chapter 11

I sleep badly, waking every two hours with bad dreams of what might be out on the wasteland. I finally get up when I hear the taxi come for Harry just after dawn. I'm not scared now. I've worked with animals all my life, and I know that all the nocturnal predators, even those in human form, go to sleep at daylight. I hate the feeling of being stalked, and it's too early for Bea to be here now, but if she was watching me last night, maybe there's some evidence?

I pull on my padded coat over pajamas and gum boots and grab my big flashlight and the broom. I creep down the front staircase quietly, so as not to disturb anyone, and walk to the area of wasteland where I heard the sound last night.

Tentatively, I approach the thick undergrowth where I thought I saw movement.

In the quiet of the morning, I can hear ragged breathing.

I squat down and shine the flashlight into the long grass underneath the bushes, keeping the bristle end of the broom pointing at the dark cave under there, in case something comes rushing out to attack me.

But it's just a big old dog lying on his side with his legs stretched out. He looks near death, but lifts his head to give a weak, rumbling growl at my approach. His matted coat is black and tan, and he looks like a German Shepherd crossed with something bigger. Around his neck is a thick leather collar with a heavy chain, and the remains of a wooden post bolted onto the end.

Somehow, this poor old boy has managed to pull the post out of the ground and drag himself here to die. Tears spring to my eyes as the dog drops his head onto the grass again in exhaustion.

"You poor old thing," I whisper. "Hang in there, boy. I'll be back."

I quickly climb back up to my apartment, find two pie pans and fill one with water. I'd bagged all the pieces of scone that Bea smashed and put them in the freezer, so now I heat some milk and use them to make a warm, soft mush. I carry it all back down and use the broom to slide the two pans close to the dog's head. "I need to go to college now, but I'll be back tonight."

I think about the old dog while I work through lectures, almost sure he'll be dead by the time I get home. At least I was able to show him some love before the end. But when I get back after five, the pans are empty, and he's still alive.

"Well, you're a fighter, no doubt about that."

The dog lifts his head a little, his sad, dark eyes meeting mine. But there's a spark of life there now that wasn't there before, and I feel hope spring inside. He's been warmed by the winter sun on the bushes all day and has managed to eat the food and water. He's backing away from death's door.

I take the pie pans and go to fill them again. Anna opens her door as I pass. "Are you feeding waifs and strays down there?"

"Only an old dog. Looks like he's been starved and beaten but I'm going to get him back on his feet. I'll take him to the rescue center, and if I can find whoever who abused him like this, I'll report them."

When I bring more food down, the dog doesn't growl.

His brown eyes watch me without malice, and I wonder at the patience of animals. After the way he's been treated, I'd expect him to attack anything on two legs.

He's still lying in the same position, but there's a lapping sound as he drinks, his chain clanking against the pan. He needs a name, and somehow, he looks like a *Bobby*.

"Good boy, Bobby." When he's finished lapping up more bread and milk, this time with lots of grated cheese in it, I take the food dish away and top up his water. Back in my apartment, I get hamburger meat out of the freezer and check to see if I have enough eggs. Tomorrow, I'll get more milk, a big block of cheese and a big bag of senior dog biscuits. I'll call the Rescue Center and the vet to see if they have any advice. I've lost too many animals from my life, and I miss them all. Bobby is going to live; I'm going to make sure of that. I make a quick evening meal, then lose myself for two hours working on the head of the stallion.

After a few more days of feeding him, I've built up enough trust with Bobby that he doesn't even growl when I touch him gently. I take photos of the state he's in, of the collar, chain, and post before I take them off. I am so angry, but I have to calm down my emotions in order not to transmit them to him. "Easy, boy, I'm not going to hurt you."

With lots of soothing reassurances and pieces of cheese as treats, he lets me gently remove everything that has enslaved him. I want to build a bonfire and burn them, but I might need them as evidence. I push them deeper into the overgrown grass, so we don't have to look at them every day. Bobby is now free, but he doesn't leave. He curls up in his grassy nest under the elderflower bush, sleeping and waiting for me each morning and evening. When I arrive now, he wags his tail and licks my hand.

Donal is a bit annoyed. "You're spending a lot of time with yon dog, Lizzie. I was hoping we'd go out some more."

"I'm sorry, Donal, but Bobby needs me. I've been putting

cream on his sores and gently grooming him. When I get him on his feet again, maybe we could take him for a walk to the beach together?"

I was going to use the fire escape to go up and down with Bobby but the iron steps are more like a ladder, and he can't manage them. Also, the clay I wedged under the fire escape door has cured the rattling, so I leave it there.

Everyone is touched by Bobby's story. As soon as he's strong enough, I bring him up the main stairs to my apartment. I give dog treats to Anna, Donal, and all the students. "When we meet on the stairs, please could you say his name in a kindly voice and give him a treat? That way he'll know you're friends."

Soon, Bobs is filling out, his sores are healing, and he's putting on weight. I get him a red nylon collar and lead as well as a shiny, silver identity tag with his name on it and my phone number. As I do the general cleaning in The Warehouse, he follows me around. I take him for a short walk in the morning and leave him in the apartment, and Anna takes him out again at lunchtime. She strokes Bobby's head now, and he licks her hand. My old boy now has two friends at least. "I never hear him bark," she says.

"He's a quiet dog generally, but I think he could be ferocious if he needed to be."

I watch out for Bea and keep the security chain in place but I'm not alone anymore, and it fills me with confidence and happiness. I hadn't realized how much I missed Jester and Pluto and the horses, the energy of animals, and I'm grateful for another creature to share my world.

As I work now, Bobby lies on his mat and listens as I tell him about Home Farm, about Dan in America and my feelings for Harry. I work the clay of my sculpture, molding, adding material, scraping it back with my special tools, constantly comparing the head that is emerging with the sketches on the wall. Bobby watches over me, and I feel safe and more at home than ever.

One afternoon, I get back from college early. "Come on, Bobs, let's go to the beach and get some of that fresh air."

After a depressing week of rain and clouds, it's a beautiful day. Bobby is on his long lead, happily wandering about and sniffing things and I turn my face into the sun, feeling the warm rays touch my skin.

Suddenly Bobby growls. A rough-looking man steps from behind a building.

He looks like a battered football player gone to seed. He stops when he sees us, and the look on his unpleasant face says he's found what he's looking for. "That's ma dog."

The hair rises all over Bobby's body, and a blood-curdling growl rips from his throat. His upper lip lifts to show massive canine teeth.

"C'mon Bobs." I pull his lead hard and sprint in the opposite direction.

The man shouts and starts to run after us, but we dash down side streets and finally, up the front steps of the police station ahead of him. I'm panting as I put Bobby into the *down* position, calming him.

"I want to file a charge of animal abuse," my voice cracks with emotion. "I found this dog abandoned and dying. I helped him. I want to claim him as mine." I'm almost sobbing now. I can't bear that a brutal man might get Bobby back and hurt him again.

The young police officer writes down my details and then points to the back door of the building. "Go that way, up the road to the Council Offices. If the dog has no license, register him and pay the fee, then he's yours."

Thanking him, I peep outside. There's no sign of the rough man, but as the door swings shut behind us, I hear the policeman speak to his colleague. "Four guard dogs, yon man's had at that car lot in as many years. This one will be better off wi' the lassie."

I get a bright yellow Council dog tag for Bobby's collar,

and he's now registered as Bobby Martin at The Warehouse address. When we come out, there's no sign of our enemy, so we celebrate with a doggy chew for Bobs and a large Americano coffee for me.

I don't feel like working when we get back to the apartment, so I make a big easy casserole in my crock-pot. I text Anna and Donal to join us for dinner. Bobby lies quietly on his mat as I serve up plates of chicken with carrots and mushrooms. Donal makes happy noises as he digs and chases dumplings in the fragrant gravy. We're good friends now that I'm cooking again.

"This tastes incredible, Lizzie. Does Bobby get any?"

Bobby wags his tail at his name, and I bend down to pat him. "Good boy. He's been fed and walked. He'll get a little taste later before bed, but I don't want him begging for human food or being aggressive while we are eating."

Anna watches as Bobs rolls over with a sigh and closes his eyes "It's amazing, isn't it? He's moving on from his past and living in the present."

I realize with a start that she could be describing me too. The Warehouse is much more of a real home now, and it's great to be here with my friends and my dog. If only Harry were here too.

Donal sighs happily as he finishes his dinner. "Lizzie, you are a wonderful woman. Will you marry me?"

I giggle as I serve up apple crumble with vanilla ice cream.

When Donal heads downstairs later, Anna stays to chat and help wash up the dishes. "I think he's serious, Lizzie. He's been hanging around, waiting for you to be free again. What happened when you went out with him that day?"

"We kissed, and it was nice." I sigh. "But is that enough to take it a step further, Anna? Donal thinks so, but I'm not sure."

She says goodnight and I lock the door behind her, then curl up on my couch with a book on making metal sculptures. Alex has asked us to research artists and methodologies ready for next semester, when we will be doing a welding course.

Bobby lies next to me on the floor and lifts his head when we hear the students below, laughing as they arrive back from the pub.

A few moments later, someone tries to open my door, rattling the doorknob. When it doesn't budge, whoever it is kicks at it with big boots and then shouts obscenities at me with slurred, drunken words.

Bea is back.

Bobby rushes to the door, barking with a deep roar of outrage. The noise bursts from his throat as he launches himself at the door. His barking is enormous, as if he intends to kill whoever dares to disturb us like this.

There's a surprised silence and the shouting and kicking stop. I quietly call Bobby to me, praise him with a big hug and a handful of treats. He's shaking all over and stands with me as she kicks at the door again.

"This place is mine, and I'll be back with a load of other people. Then we'll throw you out."

I hear running footsteps and then Harry's voice outside. "Bea? What are you doing here? What on earth is going on?"

From the ensuing exchange of high-octane expletives from both Bea and Harry, I don't get the impression that they are lovers reuniting or that he's apologizing for giving me her apartment.

I stroke Bobby's fur to make it lie flat again. He's quiet now but watches the door on full alert.

Eventually, Bea clomps off down the stairs and Harry calls through the door in an anxious voice. "Are you okay, Lizzie? For goodness sake, what's been happening?"

I don't think Bobby will let anyone else in right now, so I tell my good boy to stay, take off the security chain and slip out onto the landing. I close the door behind me and want to rush into Harry's arms, but his face is like thunder. I tell him the details of Bea's previous visit.

"But Lizzie, why didn't you tell me earlier? I could have dealt with her then."

"You had so many other things going on, and Donal put up the CCTV camera for me."

Harry huffs in annoyance. "Of course, it's always Donal to the rescue, isn't it? But I heard loud barking. Have you got a dog in there?"

I nod. "His name is Bobby. I found him on the wasteland just after you left. He was injured and sick, but he's getting better. And he's a great guard dog."

Harry shakes his head firmly, his mouth set in a hard line. "No way, Lizzie. I'm sorry about Bea and that you've felt unsafe here. But the dog has to go."

Chapter 12

Bea hasn't managed to hurt me tonight, but Harry does, and his words are like a punch below my ribs. I can barely breathe at the thought of losing my precious Bobby, and my anger explodes.

"You never think of anyone else, Harry Stewart. You're always on your own agenda."

"Lizzie, I –"

I hold up my hand, totally furious at him. "Don't say another word. You're never here, and you don't understand a thing about what's going on. Bobby is my furry Guardian Angel. I rescued him, and I'm not abandoning him now."

Harry runs his fingers through his red hair as he frowns. "It's not personal, Lizzie. It's just that the building lease doesn't allow animals. If I let you keep him, all the other tenants will have animals here too. I know Dad would say you can't keep a dog here."

My mind is whirling. After all that Bobby and I have been through, I didn't see this coming. My fragile home is shattering once again. I try to stay calm as I plead with him.

"I need him, Harry. I understand that rental leases can be difficult, but Bobby is too damaged to be adopted by anyone else. If I take him to the Rescue Center, they will put him to sleep. I want to go on living here, but if you force me to choose, then Bobby and I will leave together."

I turn and go back into my room, locking the door behind me. I lean back against it, wanting to weep, thinking of Harry's shocked face. Bobby is anxious and rubs his whole body against my legs. I kneel to smooth his head.

"It's okay, lovely boy, don't worry. You and me forever, okay?" I rest my head on top of his, and he licks my hand. "My knight in shining armor has just fallen off his horse, but it's probably time I grew up and let that fantasy go."

I curl up on the couch with him and hold him close. We both get anxious, and I remember back to when Mum used to shout at me. I do anything to avoid that kind of conflict now, and Bobby and I need peace. Harry is never here anyway, and it's Bobby who keeps me safe up here while I work or sleep. I'm not afraid when I'm with him. Bobby puts a paw on my leg, and I hold it gently. Romantic love is all very well, but we need other loves as well – family, friends, kindness, animals and good work. We need them all to survive.

I fetch my laptop and sit down again. "Looks like we need to find a new home, Bobs. But that's okay because we'll be together."

A few minutes later, I hear footsteps on the stairs, and then Harry knocks. "Lizzie, we need to talk. Please open the door."

Bobby looks up at me, and I put my finger to my lips. I give him a treat to stay silent. Harry thinks I'm still a mouse and he'll try to use his charm to persuade me to do what he wants.

After a minute or two with no response, Harry shouts in frustration. "I need to go, Lizzie. I only came back to collect equipment. I'll be back on Thursday, and maybe you'll be more logical then. You can't avoid me forever." He stomps crossly down the stairs. I hear the taxi arrive, the doors slam, and he's gone again.

I pat Bobby and grab my laptop. "Come on, old fella, let's go see Anna."

When she opens her door, there are fabric samples everywhere. "I heard the row with Bea and the storming of Harry Stewart." She raises an eyebrow and beckons me in. Then holds up a group of fabrics. "What do you think of these together?"

"Hmm, maybe a darker contrast than the second one to bring out the floral pattern?"

"Good call."

Bobs is comfortable with Anna, and he lies down quietly, nose on his paws. I put the kettle on as she works.

"So, what are you thinking now?"

I get the mugs out and open the fridge for milk. "Harry says Bobby has to go, so we need a new place to live. When I worked at the Country Club in Summerfield, there was a magazine called The Lady. Wealthy people use it to find someone to care for their big house while they travel, or other opportunities like that. There might be something similar around Edinburgh. If not, I may have to relocate again."

Anna stops sorting and looks over at me. "But what about your art course?"

I pass her coffee. "I'd hate to do it, but I won't give Bobby up. Harry thinks he'll make me change under pressure, like in the past, but Bobby needs me. I've made the decision, and I'll stick to it."

Anna warms her hands around her mug. "I'd be sorry to see you go."

"I'd miss you too." I quickly open my laptop and start searching before I get sad. "Dan and Harry used to call me Mouse because I was so small and scared of everything. But it's time to stop waiting for crumbs to fall from Harry's table."

"What about Donal?"

I turn from the screen and sigh. "Oh Anna, he's a good man, and I know he wants to take it further, but it doesn't feel like a romantic sort of love. Besides, we don't have enough in common."

Anna grins. "He's pretty hot, though."

I can't help but laugh. "Yes, definitely, but there's no spark between us. No chemistry. And I have so much going on now. Donal says that he can wait and implies that he's the opposite of Harry."

Anna shakes her head. "Och, that's just jealousy. Harry's always surrounded by women, but he works too much to find love. He runs away as soon as anyone gets too close to him."

I go back to scrolling for job opportunities. "Oh, look at this."

Anna comes to read the screen over my shoulder. "Night supervisor needed at the Airport Kennels. Accommodation provided."

"I bet they'd let me have a guard dog for night rounds." Could this be a new home for Bobby and me?

I call the kennels, and the owner introduces herself as Dianne. Her voice is warm and friendly. "Can you come for an interview tomorrow and bring Bobby with you? We're part of the Dog Protection Society and deal with a lot of rescue dogs."

Donal arrives as I get off the phone. He smiles in welcome and bends to pat Bobby. I tell him about Bea and the stand-off with Harry. "I could drive you to the kennels tomorrow if you like. I've time between jobs."

"Could you? Oh, Donal, that that would be a great help."

Harry doesn't want us. Surely, I'd be better off with a man who is interested in me and my dog, who gives up his time to be with us.

* * *

Donal drives us out to the kennels the next day, and I'm nervous but also hopeful that this might be the right place for Bobby and me. Dianne, the owner, is an older woman with dark, bobbed hair and a smiley face. Her handshake is firm, and she bends to greet Bobby. I like her already. We put Bobs into an exercise area where he can still see or hear me as we walk around. Dianne is justly proud of her well-run facility. Then we look at the small house that's attached to the quarantine kennels.

"This is the accommodation. It's basic but adequate. Bobby could live here with you. John, my husband, and I live in the house by the gate and I have three other kennel staff who live in the village nearby."

Dianne is so kind that I find myself telling her more than I intended, but it's better to be up-front. I don't like nasty surprises and know that other working folks prefer honesty. I explain the situation at The Warehouse and my art course. "I'm also already booked to go to Oxford for three days over Christmas to see Mum at the care home. Would that be okay?"

Dianne nods. "Of course. All our guest dogs are in by then so it's mostly feeding. If Bobby's not good with other males, he'll need to be in a quarantine run while you're away."

Back at Reception, she asks Bobs to sit and gives him a treat when he does. "Good dog. I think we'd work well together, Lizzie, and you are the most experienced candidate so far. Could you start this weekend? Clients are beginning to bring their dogs in for their Christmas vacation, and it's our busiest period."

I'm startled. But if I'm going to take the job, it might as well be sooner rather than later. Harry wants us out of The Warehouse, the end of my college semester is Friday, and my sculpture goes in for assessment that morning.

Dianne walks me to the gate. "The job's yours if you

want it, but it sounds like you still have some things to sort out. Could you let me know by Thursday night? If you decide not to accept, I've got two more people coming for interviews on Friday morning."

"Thanks so much, Dianne. I'll be in touch."

Back at the van, Donal opens the door for Bobby and me. "How did it go?"

"I liked her very much, and she's offered me the job."

Donal looks pleased. The kennels is stark, smells of disinfectant, and is not at all like a home, but at least I'd be standing on my own two feet, and I wouldn't owe Harry any favors.

When we get back, I give Donal a hug. "Thank you so much for taking us."

He holds me close and does not let go for a moment or two. "We'll still see each other, won't we?"

I nod, and he heads off to a job as Bobs and I climb the stairs. I give him clean water, make a cup of green tea and a sandwich for me, and then get his lunchtime snack.

Pluto and Jester, and in fact, all the Labradors we ever had at Home Farm, ate everything incredibly fast, but Bobby is a delicate eater. I'm still trying to build him up and he has full meals in the morning and at night with fortified biscuits during the day. He lies down, looking like a sphinx, following my every movement, his legs and giant paws facing forward. I place six big dog biscuits, all different colors, between his front paws.

First, he carefully sniffs each one as if he were Sherlock Holmes with a clue. Then, after much thought, he chooses one, usually the black one, and eats it slowly, focusing his whole being on this one biscuit. Every tiny crumb is searched for and licked up before he chooses the next. He's a study on living in the moment and being mindful of our blessings. I'm half-laughing at how cute he is but also worrying now about what happens to us next. I'll be tired after night duties, and it's a long way from the kennels into college. How much time will I get to do art, let alone be with Bobby?

"I've found you, dear old boy, but I may need to give up college again. What a mess! I'm in love with Harry, but he doesn't love me. Donal wants a wife, but not the new me, and besides, I'm not in love with him. Shall I just give up on the pair of them?"

Chapter 13

I'm putting the finishing touches to the stallion's head sculpture on Thursday morning when there's a knock at the door.

"Lizzie, I'm back. Can we talk?"

Harry's voice is contrite, so I wipe my hands on my apron, tell Bobby to stay, and open the door. Before I can say anything, Harry launches into an apology.

"I'm so sorry I shouted at you. I was angry at Bea and myself for leaving you in that situation. And I'm sorry about Bobby and saying he had to go. I've spoken to Dad, and he can stay as the official Warehouse guard dog. Will you stay, Lizzie, please?"

His words wash over me, and it takes a moment for them to sink in.

"Really? We can stay?"

He smiles. "Yes, please. I love coming back and finding you here. And I know he makes you feel safe. I'm so sorry about Bea. I did not, at any time, offer her this apartment, but maybe I gave her false hope when she was in prison. I should have broken off all contact with her before this. All our university mates had already done that, and I felt sorry for her isolation. Mum used to say I was always trying to save birds with broken wings."

I smile as I lead him into the apartment. "Like scrawny little kids with glasses, whose mums didn't want them."

"I still remember how you used to hide up in that chestnut tree." He walks in, and I hand him some dog treats.

"Now, may I introduce you to the official Warehouse guard dog? Bobby, come."

Bobs comes to the door and looks at me. I take Harry's hand. "Please give him a treat, Harry, and say good dog, Bobby, in a happy voice."

Harry does this and, holding hands, we practice the sit command. Harry gives Bobby the last little treat, and he settles onto his mat by the fire escape door.

"Good boy." I ruffle the fur around his neck and give him a chew toy. "Now, stay."

Harry sits on the couch as I pour tea and pass him a plate with a wedge of my coffee and walnut sponge cake. "I'm educating him carefully, so that you, Anna and Donal are part of our pack. He's never been trained, but he's so intelligent and wants to please. We just need to be clear and consistent. But thank you for letting him know you better. He's improving every day, and I sleep better with him here."

Harry bites into his cake and makes a sound of approval. "Anna told me you were offered the job at the kennels."

"Yes, and Bobs would have been an asset on night duty. But it would have been difficult to get to college, and there were other candidates, so I'll let them know I'm staying here. I'm taking the stallion's head in tomorrow."

"Can I see it again now?"

"Of course." I jump up with enthusiasm. Bobby follows us into the cold room, his nails clicking on the wooden floor. I switch on the spotlights and carefully unwrap the sculpture.

Harry walks around it and studies it from every angle. His eyes light up and I know he sees what I do in it. "It's beautiful."

"I'm glad you think so. If it survives the firing process, Alex will enter it for the sculpture scholarship. There are three Arts awards each year, and the winners get a year's tuition fees. However, there are so many good students that it's unlikely I'll win, but you never know. I want to try."

Harry helps me wrap the sculpture in its hessian cloth again, then swaddle it in bubble wrap with my name, email and phone number taped to the front. Harry helps by tearing off pieces of the sticky tape and handing them to me as I need them. "If it wins, Lizzie, we'll have it cast in bronze. Then you can truly say you started out in a drafty garret in Edinburgh."

We laugh, and it's so easy being together. He turns off the spotlights, I shut the door, and we share another slice of cake. I lick the coffee icing off my fingers and wipe them with a napkin.

"This icing is too sticky. I made another cake for Dianne, for being so nice. Hopefully, it will dry out a bit. I'm helping her over the weekend, in exchange for Bobby staying there while I'm in Oxford for the holiday."

Harry sighs. "I wish you were coming to Boise for Dan and Jenna's first Christmas. But I'll be back on the twenty-ninth. Might Dianne keep Bobby for a couple more days so that you could attend the Hogmanay Ball at the Castle with me?"

Just at that moment, I happened to be staring out at the sky, day dreaming of playing in the snow with Harry, Dan, and Jenna. His words jolt me back to reality, and I can't quite believe what I'm hearing. "What was that again?"

Harry leans forward and takes my hand. "I'm sorry that I upset you over Bea and Bobby and everything, Lizzie. Will you come to Aberdeen and meet my other family? Would you come with me to the Highland Ball?"

I want to squeal with excitement, and I can't help myself. I jump to my feet and hug him. "Oh, Harry, I'd love that.

I was so envious when Dan came to stay with you at the Castle one year. But what is the ball for? And what do I wear?"

Harry grins at my enthusiasm as he carries his plate and cup to the sink. "The Highland Ball at Hogmanay is the biggest charity event of the year. It's hosted by the Laird and his Lady on New Year's Eve, and I do the media photographs as my contribution. We all wear traditional Scottish dress, and you can rent it in town if you don't have something appropriate."

I have so many questions. Is this like a date? Or just as an apology? Is this the most romantic thing ever, or is this just Harry being nice to me like a little sister? To be honest, it doesn't matter, because I'm going to the Highland Ball!

"I can't wait! I'll talk to Anna. She knows where the shops are to get that sort of costume. But I have loads to do today before I go to the kennels tomorrow evening. Time for you to go so I can get organized."

Harry laughs and heads to the door, then turns at the last minute. "You've changed in the time you've been here, Mouse."

I take a deep breath. "That's because I'm finally making decisions about my life. And I'm no longer a mouse, Harry, so please don't call me that anymore."

"It's just a pet name, and I've always thought it was cute." His tone is playful, but I don't respond. This is deadly serious. "Okay, if you're not a mouse anymore, then what are you?"

I grin and raise my hands into claws. "I'm a lioness."

* * *

Next morning, carrying my small gifts and huge love for everyone, Harry leaves for his Christmas holiday trip to

Boise, Idaho, where Jenna and Dan now live on the Warren ranch. I go to consult Anna about clothes to wear to a Highland Ball in Aberdeen.

She's excited for me. "Not even many Scottish people get to experience that, Lizzie! I did Scottish dancing in college and was on the Exhibition team. I still have the dress and sash Mum made for me. We might have time to alter it for you. When do you leave?"

"Bobs goes with me to the kennels tomorrow, and I'm working with Dianne for the weekend. I go on from there to Oxford."

Anna nods. "My mum's on her way to Edinburgh now, and she's looking forward to meeting you. We always go to the Christmas markets together, and she's a whizz with the sewing machine. I'm sure she'd be able to alter the dress for you to wear."

Later that day, we gather in Anna's living room for a giggly girly time with dresses, and I feel so special and happy to be with them. Doreen MacDonald is warm, kind and funny, just like her daughter. I feel a pang at their obvious tenderness with each other. It was never like this with my mum, but all families have their challenges. I'm just grateful to be together with them today. Doreen tucks and pins and expertly gathers the material around me, then gives a sigh when it's done.

"Why don't I get settled in here while you two go and buy dancing slippers? I can do the sewing before Anna and I leave for London. It will be waiting to go to the ball with you when you get back from Christmas."

Anna and I jump onto a bus along Princes Street and go to a dance shop. "She's a lovely lady, your mum."

"Yes, she's something special. Remember, the sash pins to your right shoulder with the thistle brooch, Lizzie. It goes across your back and pins again on the left hip."

"Were you keen on Scottish dancing?"

Anna smiles, remembering. "I love to dance as part of both my cultures. When the docks were open, there was a big Jamaican community in Leith."

We get off the bus. "Funny, isn't it, to love Scottish reels *and* Jamaican music? We're lucky to have so many rich cultures in our lives now."

The dance store has windows full of items nestling in tinsel. I'm dizzy with the possibilities, but Anna keeps me focused. "Right. Since Duncan is the Laird, or Lord, of the castle in the country around Aberdeen, you'll need black dancing slippers … and gum boots."

"Not to wear at the same time, I hope."

We giggle and go shopping.

The day flies by and when the kennels truck comes to pick up Bobby and me, Anna and Doreen wave goodbye from their window. "Thanks, guys. Have a great time over the holiday and I'll see you in the New Year."

The two days at the kennels fly past as I learn how things are done and help Dianne with clients. When it's time to leave for the train to Oxford, I settle Bobby into a quarantine run. He has his bed, toys, and a treat but he knows something is up.

"Bobby, stay. I'll be back soon."

I shut the door that separates us and he gives an agonized howl of abandonment. I can't bear it. I want to rush in and hold him and I'm about to open the door again when Dianne puts her hand on my arm.

"If you're going to leave him with us at all, Lizzie, he must get used to this. He's scared, but as soon as he can smell that you have gone, he'll settle. Dogs have no concept of time, so he won't know if you're gone for two days or ten. Each time you leave him here, it will be easier. Go quickly now."

I'm almost in tears thinking about Bobs on the train south. I'm surrounded by families talking about heading home for Christmas, but as much as I want to see Mum, Viv and Sid, and Clair again, I feel like I'm leaving my home now, not going back to it.

Chapter 14

I finally reach Oxford. The Christmas lights are on everywhere, but my heart sinks a little as I make it to Viv and Sid's house. A Christmas tree twinkles inside, but it's not the extravagance of the Home Farm celebrations we always had when Mum was well. I would spend days in the kitchen, baking and creating, feeding people happily. It was even lovely to go to Midnight Mass at the parish church. It won't be the same this year in so many ways. Will Mum even remember those times?

But when the front door opens, Sid pulls me into a big hug, and I feel much happier. "Lizzie, you're here at last! Happy Holidays." His enthusiasm makes me smile, and then Viv comes hurrying from the kitchen, drying her hands on a towel with Pluto right behind her, his tail swishing happily. He looks at home here. Viv grabs me and holds me at arm's length, looking at my eyes. All her anxious thoughts come tumbling out.

"I've been worried about this laser surgery, dear, but your eyes look clear, are you okay, really?"

"I'm fine. I knew you'd worry, but it's all okay. Art college is everything I've dreamed of, and I can't thank you both enough for supporting me."

Viv pats my cheek. "I love the new red coat and nice boots. Looks like you have a whole new style altogether. You look quite different, love. I'll bring the tea in, and you can tell us everything you've been up to."

I bend to stroke Pluto and give him one of Bobby's soft treats from my coat pocket. "Hello, beautiful boy."

Together, we follow Sid into the sitting room where he's been reading the *Financial Times*. Pink pages are spread across the coffee table, but now he folds them neatly away for later. Viv brings in tea and a plate of her Christmas cookies.

I take my cup and saucer from Viv. "Thank you. Where's Jester?"

Sid points out the window. I can see a new enclosed run built along one side of the yard with tall posts and plastic-covered mesh. "Unfortunately, he was demolishing the house, so he's had to go outside."

All I can see is dirt flying in all directions and the rear end of a black Labrador. His head is down, and he's digging. I smile because there is nothing that Bobby likes better, either. Viv sits down with her tea and gives Pluto a piece of her cookie. "Our Jester has not settled into suburbia. He's a good dog, but a bit much for us."

"I'm going on the Boxing Day ride with Clair so I'll ask if she knows of someone around Summerfield who'd like him."

* * *

The next day is Christmas Eve, so Viv and I go shopping for groceries and small last-minute gifts. The stores in Oxford are crowded like in Edinburgh and beautifully decorated for Christmas. We go out to lunch, and I fortify myself with a glass of red wine, some Dutch courage before we go and visit Mum. I'm apprehensive about seeing her in the home, worried that she might not be happy, or whether she might be angry. It's so hard to know how she might react. So much has changed for me, and yet, she's here in the care home, a shadow of her former life.

Green Acres has made an effort for Christmas, with wreaths on the doors and a tree in the common room. It's a pleasant enough place, but it feels empty, as if the people living here have already checked out. Pluto trots along happily to Mum's room, but Viv looks weary as we walk along the corridor.

"I come here most days to feed Christine at least one meal. The nurses do a good job, but I bring some of the food she likes. And she loves to stroke Pluto. Bringing him here seems to be the one thing I can do to make her happier. But she doesn't know his name anymore." She frowns. "Perhaps she doesn't know mine anymore. I haven't asked her in a while."

I try and suppress the shudder that ripples through me. The thought of forgetting the people I love is awful. "Are we going to get like this when we're older, Viv?"

"No one knows, dear. No one knows."

When we walk in, Mum is sitting in a high-backed armchair dressed in black sweatpants and a blue sweater with a reindeer on the front. Where once her hair was flaming red and styled, it is now a salt-and-pepper mess. She smiles to see Pluto and caresses his head.

"Ahh." The sound might be a welcome, but she stares up at Viv and me, her head tipped to one side, a blank look in her eyes. I sit down on a low chair next to Pluto. "Hi Mum, Pluto and I are here to help with your dinner tonight."

Mum doesn't speak again but neither does she fuss when Viv goes. I brush her hair gently, trying to make it a semblance of what she used to like. It's all I can think of to do, and I hold back my tears, wishing for something, even a glimpse of her anger, as evidence she is still in there. But she is passive as we watch cartoons, her once capable hands resting motionless on her knees. Pluto curls up to sleep by her feet in fawn bedroom slippers, and once she's settled for bed, I leave the building and call Dan. I really need to speak to my brother. It's good to hear his voice, and I tell him how Mum is.

"I'm sorry I'm not there to support you, Liz."

"It's fine, really. I just wanted to talk. No use us both getting upset. I was just thinking of the awful night when we came to the hospital after she collapsed and you were at Summerfield with Jenna. It's shocking to see the deterioration since your wedding."

"At least she's safe and comfortable. How are things in Edinburgh?"

We catch up, and I hear sounds in the background – laughter and music. Pretending to be casual and glad he can't see my face, I ask, "Did Harry get there okay?"

"Yes, he's staying with Maggie and Greg, but we're all getting together for dinner on Christmas Day. Happy Holidays, Lizzie. Love and hugs to Viv and Sid and speak soon."

* * *

On Christmas Day, we all visit Mum again with some little gifts. She's wearing a Christmas paper hat like all the residents, but seems confused. I want to cry, so I kiss her cheek quickly and hurry outside. Viv comes out after me.

I turn, trying to hide my tears. "I'm sorry. I'm finding this so hard, but I know you come most every day. How do you stand it?"

Viv hugs me. "Don't you worry, love. I feel like this every day, and all we can do is keep coming and keep loving her."

Back at the house later, Viv gets Christmas dinner ready,

and I go for a walk with Sid and the dogs. We stroll through the Oxford water meadows, Jester snuffling through the bushes, greeting other dogs, having fun on his long lead. Sid tucks my gloved hand through his arm. He never says much, but he's a dear man and as solid as a rock. Just being with him, knowing he's there for Viv, comforts my heart. I think how reliable he has always been, even when I was a little girl.

We have a quiet Christmas with a delicious dinner and small gifts. Then we get a call from the ranch in Boise on the computer with Maggie and Greg, Jenna and Dan, and Harry on the end. I can't keep my eyes off his smiling face. They all laugh and crowd around the camera.

"Merry Christmas!"

Everyone is cheered up by talking and listening to each other across the miles and the oceans. "I heard on the news that you have heavy snow in Idaho now."

Jenna jumps in. "We sure have, Lizzie. Tomorrow, we'll drive through the pine forests up to ski and snowboard at Bogus Basin. It's only a small ski area, but it's close to Boise, and we'll have fun."

Maggie leans in and smiles at the camera. "Greg will be skiing, but I won't. I shall sit in a comfy armchair at the Lodge beside a big log fire, reading and sipping hot chocolate."

Viv grins back at our camera. "Way to go, Mags, sounds like my kind of skiing!"

Dan winds up the family call. "Happy Holidays, everyone, speak again in the New Year."

I smile to myself as the screen goes blank. In my dreams, I see myself on New Year's Eve dancing in Harry's arms. I can't wait to be back home.

* * *

After too much food and melancholy about Mum over Christmas, I am so ready for the Boxing Day ride with Clair. Viv gives me a lift in the early morning, and since we have time, we stop the car outside Home Farm, just to see it again.

Viv pats my knee. "You okay?"

I nod, surprised by how the pang of homesickness has lessened so much. "Yes, I'm fine. It's no longer my home, but I wanted to honor the memory of our life here with Mum. We had some difficult times, but there are also many happy memories."

At the Stables, light spills from the big barn. Clair comes out to hug us and Viv goes into the cottage to say hi to Ted and have a cup of tea. I'm ready to work in my favorite old jeans and my *muckers*, my short rubber boots, a red thermal roll-neck from Edinburgh and a bright green Christmas jacket with holly berries on. My hair is stuffed into my blue beanie, and Clair grins at me as we head to the feed store. "You look like an elf from Santa's Grotto."

I pull the beanie more firmly over my ears. "Mock not, I love this old hat. It used to be great for holding my glasses in place: now it's just great for keeping warm." We laugh together, and it's good to be with my best friend again.

It's a chilly but cheerful morning, and by the time Robert arrives, all the horses and ponies are ready. In the misty sunshine, excited ponies toss their heads, jingling their bits and stamping impatiently. All the riders arrive, and Robert organizes them, tightening girths and helping them mount. Clair and I hurry to change into our formal riding clothes then rush back down for the ride.

I swing up onto Teddy, one of Clair's Highland ponies. He's totally bombproof and if I need to dismount to rescue a youngster, he'll stand patiently. It's amazing to be back in the saddle.

"I've missed this." I grin across at Clair as we trot the

cavalcade to the village. Robert is in the front, as it's his first Boxing Day ride as the new Stable Manager. He looks as excited as the kids.

Clair and I manage the back of the group and the stragglers, and she looks a little down as we turn into one of the lanes. "Did you see the look on Granddad's face as we set off? He didn't want to be left behind, but age and arthritis …" She doesn't complete the sentence, but I know how she feels. It was so hard seeing Mum unable to do what she used to do so easily.

"I expect Ted will do a walk around the arena with Russ to stretch his legs then get his old deck chair and a few apples, and stay with Russ listening to the radio till we get back."

Clair nods, and we ride into the parking lot of The Potlatch Inn. It's a mass of brindled hounds and hunt staff in pink coats, horses, ponies and people. I'm glad there's no fox hunting anymore, but it's good to keep the tradition going with packs of hounds for drag hunting. A front rider starts half an hour ahead and drags a sack of scent, laying a trail for the hounds to follow. The riders follow their pack, and it's some serious fun. I lose myself in the excitement of the day, enjoying being out in the air. It's been a hell of a year.

Hours later, when everyone arrives safely back at Summerfield Stables, the day is judged a great success. That evening, Clair and I finish cleaning up and putting the horses to bed for the night. I lean on the wall by Russ's stable, watching Clair over the half-door.

My body aches, a sure sign I've not been on a horse in a long time. "I've discovered muscles I'd forgotten I had."

Clair laughs as she fills Russ's water again. He nudges her, and she strokes his muzzle. "Well, how about you stay on over the New Year? We can ride and we can go together to the New Year's Eve party at the Potlatch?"

I pause for a moment, and she glances up. "I know that look, Lizzie Martin. What are you not telling me?"

"I've been waiting for the best time to tell you, but Harry's asked me to the Highland Ball at his dad's castle." I bite my lip, waiting for her reaction.

She comes over and holds my hands. "Oh, Lizzie. I know how much he means to you. But be careful, won't you? Don't let him break your heart."

Chapter 15

Clair's warning echoes in my head as Harry and I travel north on the Edinburgh to Aberdeen express bus a week later. I understand her caution as my best friend, but I've changed since I left Summerfield, and I can enjoy this time away without getting swept into a fairytale fantasy. At least I think I can.

As I stare out the window, I listen to an old Paul Simon track, one my favorites, *All gone, to look for America*. I feel so excited, as I'm going to look for another Scotland, far beyond the gritty urban landscape of Edinburgh. There's such wild and lovely countryside outside the windows, despite the dismal weather. Unlike the day at the beach, it's not a case of me in hundreds of layers and Harry in a t-shirt. We both have on heavy jeans, hooded thermal tops, thick socks and walking boots. But I'm wearing my padded coat on the chilly bus as well.

Harry works quickly, his fingers flashing over the keys as he sends texts and emails. "I just need to confirm these arrangements, Lizzie, then I can switch off."

"Where are you going next week?"

"Paris for the fashion shows. Plus, one of my images from last year has been nominated for a media award."

"Congratulations!" I'm delighted for him, and my thoughts turn to the head of the stallion, now with Alex at college. Did it explode in the kiln? What did the other students submit? Would I ever be able to win an art prize?

Eventually, we make it to the far north. The castle owned by Harry's father and his ancestors for hundreds of years is ten miles out of Aberdeen, so we get a taxi. It's not long before it turns in between two wide pillars, a stone stag on top of each one, with a discreet sign for the hotel at the castle. We drive up a long road, running between green rhododendron bushes. Suddenly, there it is. A huge stone tower with no turrets or battlements.

"It's so different from castles in the south," I say with surprise.

Harry looks out of the window with me as we approach the great, gray granite building. "A lot of Scottish castles are like this. With only one door and no windows at ground level, a small number of clansmen could defend it by shooting arrows down on attackers. Or they could fight them off with swords at the narrow entrance." Harry points as we round the last bend. "The Great Hall and our family home are built on the back, can you see? I'll be staying there, but Fiona has reserved the nicest tower room in the hotel for you."

The taxi pulls up by the front door, and the other half of Harry's family come out to greet us. Although his mum, Maggie, is my godmother and I know his sister, Sam, I've never met his dad or his step-mother and half-siblings. Two enormous deerhounds bound about, and a wee black Highland Terrier runs around our legs, all barking enthusiastically.

Duncan Stewart, Harry's dad, is a stocky, gray-haired man wearing a well-worn kilt, knee socks, and brogues. We shake hands, and I'm warmed by his smiling blue eyes, so like Harry's. "A pleasure to meet you, Lizzie. This is my wife, Fiona, and our children, Jamie, Heather and Rob."

Fiona is in her fifties, taller than me, with a strong hand-shake. She looks efficient with iron-gray hair cut in a short, modern style. Her tweed midi-skirt and vest over the brown boots look suitable for greeting guests and doing practical jobs. Her direct look appraises me as we shake hands and I wonder what she's thinking.

I shake hands with Jamie, Heather, and Rob and we all go in for tea. Heather sits next to me on one side, her shoulder-length auburn hair just a shade lighter than Harry's. She chats easily. "I'm in my final year at the university in Aberdeen doing Business Studies. I'm hoping to join Mum in the hotel management when I graduate. Rob is a senior in high school."

Rob leans around her to grin at me. "And I'm not at all into the estate or the business."

She makes a face at him. "He wants to be an engineer."

"Which he could do here," Duncan joins in the conversation, "and be useful to the family."

"Nah, Dad. I'm talking engineering, as in commercial space flight, not combine harvesters."

On my other side, Jamie laughs and offers a plate of homemade shortbread. He's the same age as me and tells me how he runs the farm on the Castle Estate, managing the outdoor activities for guests like fishing and pigeon shooting.

Heather looks over at Harry, now in deep conversation with Fiona and Duncan. "Have you finished your tea, Lizzie? Shall I show you to your room?"

"That would be great."

We stand up, and she waves over at Harry, indicating that we're going upstairs. Harry comes over for a moment. "Thanks, Heather. Jamie and I are going out in a few minutes. Come with us, Lizzie? But bring your gum boots, it's muddy."

In the hallway, I admire the beautiful, soft furnishings

and dark paneling which remind me so much of Home Farm. Heather opens a door on the landing at the top of the stairs, and I follow her into a fabulous bedroom.

"Mum and Dad invested in a complete makeover about two years ago. Since then, we've focused on a small number of guests for exclusive vacations or honeymoons."

The deep, wool carpet is soft green and surrounds an enormous four-poster bed hung with rich tapestry drapes in green and cream. There are fresh flowers on the writing desk by the window and outside the loch sparkles in a sudden burst of evening sunshine.

"Oh, it's lovely."

"Harry says you're an artist, so we reserved this room for you. It has a medieval painted ceiling like the one in the Grand Hall where we'll dance tonight. All the colors are matched to original landscapes in the library."

I smile, a little embarrassed. "Well, I'm only just starting out as an art student, but thank you, I love the room."

"Then I'll leave you to settle in. Come down again when you're ready to go out with Harry and Jamie."

I turn from the window to smile at her and blurt out the question I've been dying to ask. "Do Harry's girlfriends usually stay in this room?"

Heather looks puzzled and then she grins. "Ah, Harry's wicked reputation. Then you'll be surprised to know that you're the first woman Harry has ever brought here. And you're his friend Dan's sister, that's why it's so special."

She closes the door behind her, and I take a deep breath. Am I special to Harry? And is it only because I'm Dan's sister?

After the austerity of my cold bathroom and everyday life at The Warehouse, I savor the luxury of my room. It smells of honeysuckle, and the huge bathroom has a pile of fluffy towels, a thick white toweling bathrobe, and designer toiletries. There's a tempting box of local, handmade chocolates on my pillow. I feel as if I've stepped back into history but with all the modern comforts. I quickly hang Anna's dress in the closet and freshen up after the journey, then change and head downstairs.

Harry's now wearing a kilt and a tweed jacket with leather patches on the elbows. He stands with Jamie, and they share a good laugh about my pale blue, spotted gum boots. I grin. "I don't care what you think, boys. They're more fun than your boring old green ones."

Harry takes my hand to help me slide into the bench seat of an old Land Rover, while Jamie loads the deerhounds in the back. Then Harry focuses on driving, but the vehicle bucks like a wild horse along the rough track. There are no seat belts, and since Jamie's arm rests along the back of the seat behind me, I grab hold of it to stay steady. He laughs and puts his arm around my shoulder, holding me tight against him, pointing out things of interest as we pass.

"We do three-day Highland pigeon shooting," Jamie explains. "See the hides just there? We have them camouflaged in natural surroundings all over the estate. Where exactly are you heading, Harry?"

"Dad is working with Fi, checking things for tonight. He asked me to go over the new lease with one of the tenants."

Jamie points to a clearing ahead. "You can handle that then. Can you let Lizzie and me out here? I'll show her our herd of prize-winning Black Angus, and you can pick us up on the way back."

It sounds preferable to tenant related business, so Jamie and I hop out with the deerhounds and Harry drives on. It's getting colder, and I turn my collar up against a rising wind that smells of rain. We walk across the tussocky grass as the dogs hunt through the gorse for rabbits ahead of us. At the river, we turn upstream.

"This is the tributary that runs through the estate. With careful conservation, we can provide fishing access to five hundred salmon a year." Then Jamie points ahead, and I see the herd. Black Aberdeen Angus cows, heifers and bullocks, all in different fields along the track. "These are my beauties."

We stand with one foot on the bottom rung of the gate, our arms along the top. Just how I used to stand and watch our ponies. We study the cattle, and he reaches over to scratch the head of a bullock at the gate. They crowd around us, curious and eyeing the dogs.

"They are magnificent, Jamie. In tip-top condition."

He looks pleased. "They fetch a premium commercially, but they're also a delight to keep. I got hooked on the Angus Youth Program at age fourteen. Prince Charles is the patron of our Society and has a successful herd." He grins, relaxed and happy with his cattle. It's fascinating to see a glimpse of what life is like up here. Part of me is happy to be back in the countryside, and it's wonderful to meet Harry's family, but I'm pleased when we hear Harry returning with the truck, especially as the rain starts to pour down. We race each other along the track, me sloshing in my little boots, as Jamie laughs at me. The dogs bound after us as sheets of rain slant across the landscape.

As we walk across the yard to the family house at the back of the Castle, Harry takes my hand and draws me close to his side. I hang up my wet coat, and we change our boots. In the family kitchen, Fiona looks harassed as she scrolls down her phone.

She looks up as we come in. "Sorry, dears, I'm so distracted. One of the key staff has called in sick, and Chef is throwing a tantrum in the hotel kitchen. They're short-staffed in preparing the buffet for the ball."

"Can I help at all? I'm an experienced baker."

Fiona looks relieved. "Oh, would you? That would help so much. An extra pair of hands might be just enough to stop the meltdown."

Harry takes my hand. "Text Chef that we're coming over and I'll take Lizzie to meet him."

He guides me along the different corridors that run under the castle and as we draw near to the kitchen, Harry stops in a shadowy nook and pulls me gently into his arms. My heart leaps as he gently touches my lips with his. The electricity zaps between us. "It's so good of you to help when you're meant to be on holiday. I'll come back later to fetch you: otherwise, you'll get lost in there."

He introduces me to Chef and the kitchen staff, I scrub my hands, don white cap and apron and start helping with whatever I can. It feels good to be cooking again, just like old times at Home Farm. The team chats happily while we work, and I soon know all their names. When Harry returns, Chef is carving venison, and we're putting the finishing touches to the dinner service.

"Thanks for helping out, Lizzie. Come and see us again soon."

Harry guides me back to my room through the passage-ways. "Samantha and I used to play hide and seek down here with Jamie and Heather when we were kids. The castle has a whole warren of underground tunnels dating back a hundred years or more. Very useful for getting from one part to another without going outside."

On the way, he stops at one of the bars and pours a glass of champagne for me. "For you to relax with before the ball. I'll join you in a glass later, once you come back down." At my door, he kisses my hand and leaves me to change. I still feel the touch of his lips on my skin as I start to get ready.

The wine gives me the confidence to put on the delicate white Scottish dance dress, apply light makeup, do my hair, and then venture down the main stairs again. I hope to goodness that I'm wearing the right things. I'm so grateful to Doreen, as the dress fits perfectly and feels as if it was made for me alone.

The dinner gong sounds.

Fiona and Heather smile as I walk to join them. They both look elegant in similar white dresses with black dancing slippers. Duncan, Harry, and Jamie all look amazing in Clan Stewart dress kilts matched with short black jackets, white frilled shirts, and black knee socks. I know that the pouch, worn around the waist on a silver chain, is a *sporran.* Anna told me that the dagger in the top of their sock is called a *sgian-dubh,* Gaelic for a small hidden knife.

"You look beautiful," Harry says softly as he comes forward to offer his hand and guides me into the dining hall. He sits me next to him at the dining table. Jamie sits opposite and he leans forward as he unfolds his linen napkin. "Fiona and Heather are wearing Stewart sashes, Lizzie, but yours is the MacDonald tartan."

There's a teasing look on his face, and I'm puzzled. "I don't belong to a Clan, so I borrowed the outfit from my friend, Anna. It's her father's tartan."

Jamie shakes his head. "Oh dear, that's unfortunate, because the MacDonalds are our sworn enemies. Now that you are inside our castle, tradition says that Harry must kill you … or marry you."

Chapter 16

"Jamie!" Fiona raises her eyebrows at him as I drop my head in embarrassment.

"Sorry, Lizzie, it's like this all the time when these two get together. You'll have to forgive my son for being crass." She shoots him a warning look. "Pass the bread, Jamie, please."

I don't look at Harry and focus on my dinner. First, a tasty, vegetable soup accompanied by my crusty whole-grain bread, then homemade pork pies made by Chef with salad.

"And a special vegetarian pie for Lizzie." Fiona passes my plate, and at last, she sits down. "From Chef, with love. He's on track again because you helped them out."

Duncan smiles at me. "Thanks for your help. Eat up. You'll need lots of energy for dancing."

After that, dinner is relaxed and comfortable until, high on the Castle walls, a piper begins to play. He's welcoming guests to the Hogmanay Ball, and I thrill to the sound. We get up from the table, and Harry offers his arm to escort me to the Great Hall.

We descend the wide oak staircase together into the Great Hall. Harry squeezes my hand and bends to whisper in my ear.

"Your eyes are sparkling so bright, Lizzie. You look like a beautiful maiden from medieval times. I'm on photo duty now, so I've asked my family to make sure you dance. But you'll save one or two for me, won't you?"

I go to stand quietly in the shadows at the side to watch people greet Duncan and Fiona as they enter. I love the lilt of Scottish voices and the joyful sound of a dance band warming up. On the low stage at one end of the hall are fiddles, pipes and drums. At the opposite end is a huge stone fireplace, big enough to burn a tree, but tonight it's full of flowers. All the men wear kilts in their different Clan tartans, and the women are in white dresses like mine with sashes to match the kilts. It feels like the set of a Highland movie, but it's the real thing!

Duncan steps up onto the stage to welcome the guests, and everyone falls silent as he officially opens the Hogmanay Ball. Then people take their partners for the first dance, forming square sets up and down the hall as serving staff bustle around with drinks on trays. White and tartan reflect on the polished wooden floor, and I'm thrilled to be in the middle of such pageantry.

Jamie bows in front of me. "Would ye care to dance, Lizzie?"

"I'd love to, but only if you promise not to tease me anymore."

"Of course. I'm sorry for upsetting you at dinner, but you should have seen Harry's face!" He chortles with laughter as he leads me to a place in the set, then looks over his shoulder to see what I'm staring at. The wall behind him is covered with swords and shields. "They're for fighting if anyone attacks us while we're dancing."

Jamie bows and I curtsey. My pulse races as he partners me in the Eightsome Reel. In Scottish dancing, you hold hands with your partner and smile into their eyes. You keep contact as you dance, parting and coming back together again. As I dance to the glorious Scottish music without worrying about my glasses fogging up or falling off, I thank heaven for the miracle of laser surgery. Jamie swings me around the corners until I'm breathless, my face flushed from the dance as the final notes end. We curtsy and bow.

"Thank you so much, Jamie."

"I'll come and find you for another dance later."

He bows again, and I glance over at Harry and catch a look in his eyes that makes me giggle. He's jealous! I feel so alive, confident and happy. It will do Harry Stewart good to see that I'm not the mouse he used to watch scurrying away from the light. Lots of men want to dance with me, and I say yes to them all, whirling around as the music lifts me higher. Who needs champagne when you have Scottish dancing!

I partner with Duncan and I see Harry in his dad as we dance. What a handsome family they are. But the next dance is a complex one, so I stop for a rest while Duncan dances with Fiona and Jamie partners with Heather. You can see that they're siblings. Not just in the similar auburn hair and blue eyes but in their faces and figures. They are both great dancers, obviously well used to partnering with each other. They leap high and twirl, grinning at each other as everyone whoops and claps along with the reel.

Then it's time for the band to take a break, and Fiona and Duncan lead everyone into the next room for refreshments and buffet. I know that, as hostess, Fiona is always on duty. In the kitchen, I heard whispered remarks about her acid tongue under stress, and it reminds me of working at the country club. All calm and under control around the guests while the staff paddle like crazy underneath just to keep up.

Harry joins me with Jamie, and we all clink glasses. Several glamorous women move in to join us too, flirting with both men. Harry introduces me as his friend in between their requests for photographs and the names of magazines that might publish them.

I finish my drink and slip away to place it on a side table. I'm still feeling hot, so I duck through a nearby door onto the terrace and draw in a lungful of winter air. The sound of the party fades behind me as I look out into the night. It feels like we're pushing back the darkness of winter with our celebration. I tread carefully on the frosty flagstones as I tiptoe to the edge, but when I start to feel the chill curl into my bones, I turn back to retrace my steps.

But in the darkness, I can't find the door. It must have swung shut. I rub my arms as I try to find it. I'm just starting to panic when suddenly the door opens further along the building, and the shadows are driven away by the light.

Harry looks around the corner. "Lizzie, what are you doing out here? Come in quickly. It's our dance."

I reach out to grasp Harry's outstretched hand, and he leads me back into the warm and out onto the dance floor. Where he was once a gangly teenager, he's now a handsome man with short red-gold hair and the designer stubble favored by the fashion world. Harry's kilt swings as he walks onto the floor and every woman in the room gazes after him.

With my hand in his, and my white dress flowing around my legs, Harry and I partner in a perfect Strathspey. As we flow through the movements, we gaze into each other's eyes, and I want to stay dancing with him forever. But at the final chord, the first stroke of midnight rings out from the castle clock. Everyone rushes to join hands in one big circle, and we count down.

"Five … four … three … two … one. Happy New Year!"

Harry wraps his arms around me and kisses me full on my lips, lingering for barely a moment. Then his family surrounds us, and we break apart to embrace other family members, and we wish each other a Happy New Year. The band strikes up the notes of Auld Lang Syne, and everyone crosses their arms and joins hands again to sing together.

Should auld acquaintance be forgot.

It's a nostalgic song carried by Scottish people as they emigrated worldwide. At the end of the old year and the start of the new, it's sung to remember old friendships and to think of home. I'm far away from my family, and I think of Dan and Jenna in Idaho and Viv, Sid and Mum in Oxford, Clair in Summerfield, and Bobby in Edinburgh. My heart is split over so many places now.

Then I look over at Harry, his face alight with happiness. Perhaps most of my heart is here, after all.

It's the end of a magical evening, and I stand with Harry and his family as guests bid farewell to the Laird and his Lady. When everyone has gone, Harry escorts me up to my room. As we climb the stairs, hand in hand, my heart is thumping with desire, and suddenly the chemistry between us becomes too much.

On the landing, Harry pulls me into his arms and I go willingly. His eyes are dark with desire and there's a hunger in both of us we can no longer deny. We kiss as if we'll never stop, slow, sweet kisses that set me on fire, then he draws back a little to run one tender finger down my cheek. I take it in my hand and kiss it, so full of love for him.

"The little girl who hid in the chestnut tree has grown into an incredible woman."

He kisses me again, and I revel in the strength of his arms around me.

"Lizzie, I need to tell you –"

The sound of footsteps comes up the stairs toward us, and we break apart like guilty teenagers.

Fiona stops as she sees us. "Oh, I'm so sorry, my dears, I didn't know you were here. But now I've found you, Harry, your dad's snoring in his recliner. He's exhausted. Could you give me a hand locking up? You know it takes a while after events."

"Of course, Fi." Harry smiles and squeezes my fingers. "Sleep well, Lizzie, I'll see you at breakfast."

He heads off down the stairs, and Fiona turns to me, her face lined with fatigue.

"I'm so sorry to interrupt you, Lizzie, but I really need the help." She rubs at her temples, and I see stress in the lines on her face.

"Are you okay?"

Fiona sighs. "This used to be more fun, but these days being the Laird and his Lady is hard work. Duncan is ten years older than me and has been diagnosed with a heart condition."

I put a hand on her arm. "Oh, I'm so sorry to hear that." Harry hasn't mentioned his father's health issues but I know how difficult it will be for him.

Fiona nods. "Hopefully, he won't have to take the strain much longer. He and I have agreed that he will retire soon and announce his successor at the Spring Ball in March. The title, the castle and all its lands follow the male line. As Duncan's eldest son, Harry will be the next Laird."

Chapter 17

Fiona's words are still ringing in my ears as we board the bus down to Edinburgh the next day. Harry is no longer relaxed, but back in his professional world as he answers emails about his next trip. I want to talk about what happened, but he is clearly thinking of work and leaving for France tomorrow. He's distracted, with no mention of what happened between us.

I gaze out the window, thinking of the light-hearted banter at breakfast with his family and Duncan driving us back to the bus station, pulling away with a wave, with the head of a deerhound sticking out of the passenger window. Will I ever go there again?

The sparkle of New Year's Eve is over, and I'm trying to adapt to a different understanding of Harry's destiny. Of course, he's been coming to the castle for summer vacations and every Christmas since he was three, but he has never mentioned his possible inheritance to Dan or me. But who could resist the magnificence of living here, being the Laird and running a great estate?

I'm more suited to the kitchen and the back stairs, and I'm angry at myself for making romantic assumptions. It hurts to feel like a fool. At The Warehouse, Harry was sorry for what happened with Bea and hurting me over Bobby, so he was kind to make up for it. No big deal for sophisticated Harry Stewart and his kisses were just a moment of escape. He must get opportunities to kiss a lot of women. I turn my back on him to look out the window.

Harry finishes his emails and touches my arm. "You alright this morning?"

His blue eyes are earnest, apologetic, but there's so much between us now. "Were you ever going to tell me about you becoming the next Laird?"

His face flushes, and he looks annoyed. "Fiona shouldn't have said anything about that. It's family stuff. But since you already know." He sighs. "Frankly, it's been a shock to me. Dad never said a word about his heart condition until this trip. Of course, we've always joked about the inheritance. Jamie reckons he'd make a better Laird and tells me so at regular intervals. But Dad admires the Queen. Like her, he's always said that he's in the job for life, so I never expected anything to happen for many years." He stares beyond me out the window. "And I just don't know if I can see myself living there. It's never been my home."

He runs his hands through his hair, and his frown deepens. "I guess I have a lot of thinking to do."

There seems to be nothing more to say, and I'm sleepy. I shut my eyes and lean against Harry. He slides his arm around my shoulders and makes me more comfortable. I drift off, eventually feeling his head rest on top of mine. For now, we are friends again, but I won't expect anything more. It was just a Highland fling.

Back at The Warehouse, I reach up to give him a peck on the cheek. "Thank you for a unique experience, Harry. Meeting your family, seeing the Castle and dancing at the Highland Ball are all amazing things that I'll never forget."

I don't mention the midnight kisses.

"I'm away early tomorrow, so I'll see you when I'm back from France, okay?"

As I climb the stairs to my apartment, the old song echoes in my heart. *For auld lang syne, my dear, for auld lang syne.* Is Harry just an old acquaintance that I should forget now and move on?

At least there's one boy in my life who is 100% committed to me. I grab a sandwich from the store next to the taxi stand and pay double the fare for him to take me to pick up Bobby from the kennels. When Dianne brings him into the yard, he's bouncing like a puppy, and I laugh to see him.

"That's the first time I've seen him doing that. Has he grown? He looks bigger."

I give my good boy small cubes of cheese, a favorite treat but one he rarely gets because of the high fat.

Dianne smiles. "He let out that one long howl when you left and has been silent ever since. But when he heard your voice just now, he tore around in circles barking like a mad thing."

As if on cue, Bobby begins his happy barking again. "He's telling me it's time to go to the beach!"

As we climb out of the taxi at The Warehouse, Anna arrives back from the train station and her Christmas vacation in London. She's surrounded by bags and just opening the door to her apartment. Bobs and I rush up to give her hugs.

"Happy New Year!"

"We just got back as well and I need to take Bobs for a walk after all that time in the kennels."

"Okay, then come in for hot chocolate on the way back, and we can catch up on all the news. I've been dying to hear about the ball, Lizzie. Just quickly, give me a little report. How was it?"

I take a deep breath. "Totally fabulous. Thanks to you and Doreen, I felt wonderful in the dress. I fitted right in and danced all night."

She raises an eyebrow. "And Harry?"

I shrug and bend to pat Bobs. "Same old, same old. Hot and then cold again. Between you and me, Duncan is going to retire and Harry will be the next Laird. They're having a family meeting when he gets back from France."

Anna looks impressed. "Wow! He's joked about it in the past but never as a reality. Oh, and there's big news on the Donal front as well. He swung by just after you left to tell me pointedly that he's dating someone else. I think I'm supposed to let you know."

Bobby pulls on his lead. "That's good. Maybe now we can just be friends. Gotta go, back soon."

I head out for a brisk walk along the estuary path, my happy dog at my side. It's good to be together again. The sea and sky are their usual gray, darkening even earlier in the January chill, but the wind is fresh, and there are gulls joyriding above us on the wind. I think about Harry and my heart aches. Clair will know what to say to comfort me, but I won't mention about the Laird thing until it's formally announced. If she mentioned it to Ted, and somehow it got out in Summerfield, Harry would never forgive me. I shouldn't even have blurted it out to Anna like that.

Bobby stops to digs a hole, whining with happiness, so I sit down in the shelter of a breakwater and call Clair.

"Happy New Year!"

"Hey, Happy New Year to you too! How did it go at the Castle?"

"It was brilliant, and Harry kissed me as the New Year turned. It's like he felt something, too, Clair, but back in Edinburgh, he just ran away again. I thought we were getting somewhere, but now I'm losing faith."

Clair sighs. "Perhaps we need to give up our romantic dreams of Mr. Right? Kyle is really annoying me at the moment."

"Or just be happy on our own? Of the two men I currently know with any romantic possibilities, Donal wants a trophy housewife and Harry plays too many emotional games."

Bobs comes back, covered in sand. He lies down, as close as he can get to me and I stroke his ears. "But wouldn't it be great to be married to someone who loves you, to have a home and family someday? I can't do that with someone who is terrified of commitment like Harry Stewart."

"What happened with Donal then? He didn't sound afraid of commitment."

Bobby darts off to chase a cheeky seagull. "Anna said he met someone else over Christmas and I'm happy about that. We didn't have enough in common anyway. But is being married to someone like Donal better than waiting for Harry? I'd only need to be a good cook, run a home and please his mother. But that's so –"

"BORING!" We both shout it together and shriek with laughter.

"Thank goodness for you, Lizzie. I'd go crazy if I couldn't talk to you and tell the truth to someone. If you ever do get it together with Harry, at least you'll never be bored."

"Fascinated, infuriated, but never bored."

"Maybe you need to be more fascinating and infuriating around him?"

"I don't know how to play those games, and I don't want to. I'm going to focus on my art, enjoy Bobby and have fun with my friends. I just wish you weren't so far away. College starts again on the twelfth, and I'm on a welding course for metal sculptures. So men are totally off the agenda."

"Right, Granddad's calling and I need to go. I'll call tomorrow for a longer chat."

As we talked, I hadn't noticed the darkness creeping in across the water or icy flecks on the wind, but now I realize how cold and miserable it is out here. Time to head home. I stuff my phone deep into my pocket and turn for the walk back, looking forward to hot chocolate with Anna. I can't change the way I feel about Harry. Whatever happens in the future, I'll always remember the Hogmanay Ball, because he kissed me and I felt beautiful that night.

"Come on, Bobs, ready for your dinner? Time to get started on the New Year."

But when I open the front door of The Warehouse and unclip Bobby's lead, we are both suddenly alert.

An unusual wind blows down the stairs. Something is wrong.

Chapter 18

Bobs and I race up the stairs, and as we pass Anna's door, I bang on it. "Help, Anna!"

Holding my side and panting, I sprint the last two flights and reach my landing. Bobby is already there, whining and scratching at the door. Then he barks, loud and angry. I fumble with my keys.

"Come on, come on!"

I finally manage to get the door open. It swings wide, and my hand flies to my mouth. My lovely home is a mess of graffiti in angry red aerosol paint. There are foul words sprayed in crimson all over the couch and kitchen, the once-white walls and billowing drapes. A pane of glass has been smashed inwards, and the door to the fire escape is wide open.

Bobby launches himself across the room as the sounds of boots clomp down the metal steps outside. Bobby runs out after them.

"Get her, Bobs! Anna, call the police!" I race after Bobby. It's now completely dark, but I see Bea's broad figure under the street lamp ahead. Bobby reaches the bottom of the fire escape and bounds after her, grabbing a mouthful of her skirt as she starts to run.

She swings around, screaming at him, hitting him with her fists, trying to kick him away. "Get off me, you little –"

"Good boy, hold on. The police are coming."

I reach them, and Bea curses me, raising a clenched fist to punch me in the face.

Bobby jumps. He's not a trained police dog, but his jaws fasten on her arm. The weight of his big furry body knocks her backward, and she falls onto the rough ground. With his teeth locked on her arm, he plants his front feet as she tries to roll. He growls, and I go to help him.

Suddenly, a car engine revs nearby.

Headlights shine on full beam into my face, and I'm blinded as the car roars toward us. At the very last moment, it swerves and deliberately slams Bobby with the front bumper. He's knocked off Bea, taking a chunk of her arm as he is thrown against the wall.

Bea screams at us as she scrambles head first into the open passenger door, blood pouring from her arm. The driver screeches into a high-speed turn and races off.

"Bobby, Bobby!" I kneel by my boy, and I know he is badly injured. Tears run down my cheeks as his dark eyes flutter closed. He gives a little whine of pain as Anna reaches us. I look up at her. "We need to get him to the vet right now."

Anna points to an old wood panel that's been behind the trash cans forever. "We can use that and carry him. It's the fastest way."

Carefully, we lift Bobby onto the panel. We each grab an end and stagger along the path as fast as we can, through the gap between the buildings and down the high street to the vet. Thank goodness, the vet's surgery still has a light shining in the window.

"Help, please help!" I shout and frantically ring the doorbell. The sound of hurrying feet comes along the hallway, and the door opens.

Graham, Bobby's vet, takes one look at him. "Around the back."

Near to collapse with the strain, Anna and I manage to get the panel with Bobby on it into the operating room. With Graham's help, we lower it gently onto the floor. Bobby doesn't move, and his eyes are still closed.

Graham puts on his surgical gown and points. "Wait outside, Lizzie. I need to look at him." He puts a hand on my arm. "You know I'll do everything I can."

Anna gently tugs on my arm. "Come on. It might be a long wait."

I sit down on a hard chair in the waiting room, elbows between my knees, head in my hands. I feel like throwing up. "I should have just let her go. I was so angry. I shouted at Bobby to get her. Now he may die because of me."

"Drink this." Anna hands me a plastic cup. "Coffee, two sugars. You're in shock. Drink up."

I don't know how long we sit there waiting, but I jump to my feet when the door opens.

Graham looks grim and shakes his head. "It's bad news, I'm afraid. His spinal cord is severed. Bobby won't ever walk again."

For an insane moment, I picture those little harnesses with wheels for small dogs with spinal injuries. But Bobby is big with great dignity and a noble spirit. I could not put him through that, even to keep him here with me.

Graham continues. "With his injuries, Lizzie, he'll be in a lot of pain even if he makes it." He shakes his head. "You did an amazing job with him. He was broken when you found him, but you patched him up well. You gave him another life, Lizzie, but this is one injury too many. You need to let him go."

His words chill me, but I know that if Bobby were in the wild, he'd die slowly and in pain with this injury. I must be brave and do the right thing for my boy. I must hold him safe in my arms as he goes home.

Anna takes the coffee cup from my frozen fingers. "Shall I come in with you?"

I shake my head as the tears start to come. "Thanks, but I need to do this on my own."

Graham leads me into the operating room. "He regained consciousness when I was examining him. He's sedated now and in no pain, but his back legs are paralyzed."

Bobby has always been too big to get onto a table, and he lies on his side on a sterile sheet on the floor. His lower half is covered with another sheet. "Thanks, Graham."

At the sound of my voice, Bobby's eyes fly open, and he scrabbles with his front paws trying and get up. I'm next to him in a moment. "Stay, Bobs." I lay a gentle hand on his head and stroke his silky ears. His face relaxes to see me. "Good boy, Bobby. Rest now."

"It needs to be done soon, Lizzie." Graham squats beside me. "Send him off peacefully with your voice the last thing he hears."

He shaves a patch on Bobby's front paw, and I see the long needle in a kidney dish on the countertop. Graham stands up to get it, and I'm suddenly panic-stricken.

"Wait." My heart pounds. "Graham, I'm not ready. I can't bear to lose him."

Graham sighs heavily. "This is the worst part of my job, Lizzie. But Bobby is heavily sedated. This small amount gives him an overdose and everything stops. He needs to go, so make a fuss of him now."

I lift Bobby's head and slide my legs underneath. Then I wrap my arms around the strong body and kiss the soft fur. I look deep into those beautiful brown eyes that look back at me with love. "Good boy. I love you so much, Bobs."

Graham moves closer, and it is done. There's no pain, and a moment later, Bobby's spirit is gone from his eyes, and his head is a dead weight, heavy on my leg.

My Bobby has gone home, but he will always be in my heart.

At that moment, I have an overwhelming need for Harry, like when we were young, and I was hurting. My kind friend, who hides his sensitivity behind a camera lens. Because it's a tough world and when you open yourself to love, you also open your heart to be hurt. But Harry's in France and I can't ask him to help me anymore.

Anna comes in to say goodbye to Bobby, and we both weep at losing him. With a last backward look at his still body under the sheet, I go into the office with Graham and arrange for him to be picked up by the Pet Crematorium.

Then Anna and I walk home. The streets are empty. There is no dog trotting beside me. Anna links her arm through mine and I can't help the sobs.

"Come and sleep at my place. You shouldn't be on your own tonight, and we can clean up your apartment together tomorrow."

I shake my head. "Thank you, but I don't think I'll be able to sleep. I want to clear it up and do something practical. Tomorrow morning, I'll go away for a few days. I need time to clear my head."

She gives my hand a squeeze as we arrive back at The Warehouse. "If you're sure, but come down if you need me. I loved Bobby too, you know that."

We are both crying again. What happened here tonight seems impossible, and I expect to hear Bobby bark at any moment.

"Thanks for being such a great friend, Anna."

I mount the stairs with feet like lead, then push open the door to what used to be a home for Bobby and me. But there's no click of claws on the wooden boards as he comes to welcome me, no cold nose against the back of my leg. I try not to read the foul words sprayed on the walls, but the scarlet paint mocks and insults me.

I pack everything that's not touched with graffiti into boxes. My winter clothes go into the big suitcase on wheels so I can take them away. My passport and keys go into my backpack. I look at my phone where my favorite pictures of Bobby are. I look at one with his ears flopped back and a joyful doggy smile on his face. Tears threaten again, and I wipe them away.

I carefully take down the white gossamer curtains, folding them inwards so as not to get smeared with red paint. I stuff them into black trash bags with the ruined cushions, Bobby's sleeping mats, towels, and bowls. Cleaning up helps me to push the hurt down inside, and when I finish, it's beginning to get light outside.

My first dawn without Bobby; but the world continues to turn, and life goes on, regardless. However, I need somewhere safe to grieve, and this place is not safe anymore. I wish I could go back to Summerfield, to a life less complicated, but my home there is gone. I could go to Clair's or Viv's, but I just want to be alone while I weep. Then I remember Maggie's Square Cottage, always available to family members who want to stay there. Selena from The Potlatch next door manages it while Maggie's away, so I call her as the sun comes up. I know she'll be up baking or working in her garden.

Sure enough, she answers on the second ring.

My voice cracks when I tell her about what happened. She's also lost beloved animals and understands.

"I'm so sorry, Lizzie, and of course, you can stay at Square Cottage. Maggie and Greg are in the US right now. They'd be happy to know you came when you needed some peace and quiet time."

"Could you keep it quiet, Selena? Not tell Clair or Viv or anyone, just yet? I just need to be on my own."

"Absolutely. Safe journey and come in for the keys when you get here."

I'm numb as the train pulls out of Edinburgh and I spend the journey south just staring out the window. So much has changed again in the last few days. The magnificent high of the Hogmanay Ball and the devastating loss of my dear Bobby.

When I finally make it to Summerfield, Selena takes one look at me and gives me a big hug. "Oh, you poor dear. Things will look better after you sleep." She puts the keys to the cottage into a little basket with some muffins and a carton of milk for tea. "Let me know if you need anything, but come over for dinner tonight. Okay? If you don't come, then I'll be over to find you."

When I open the front door of Square Cottage, it's warm and smells of Maggie's rose potpourri and lavender. It's comforting and familiar. I can breathe more easily surrounded by happy memories of being here. I close the drapes in the sitting room so that no one can see in, then I sit in the big kitchen chair next to the Aga stove and sip a mug of tea. I let warmth seep into me as the clock on the wall above me tick-tocks a regular beat. I was last here with Harry, but he has never loved me unconditionally like Bobby did, and now it's my fault that Bobby is dead.

I want my scruffy old German Shepherd back. I put my head against the warm stove, and my muffled howl of misery echoes through the cottage, like my dog, feeling abandoned at the kennels.

After my tears dry again, I lock up and slowly haul myself up the stairs and take a warm shower, before falling exhausted into Maggie's guest bed. I toss and turn, but I must have fallen asleep at some point because I dream of Bobby. He is so close that I can touch him. We sit on the floor playing the 'give me your paw' game. Bobs was afraid of having his paws held so we played this game regularly with lots of treats so he'd be okay at the vet's office.

"Give me your paw. Good boy. Now the other paw – other paw – good dog."

I can feel the weight of his paws, and his eyes are shining as he enjoys the game and the treats. I slowly wake, feeling a little bit comforted. I think of Bobby and realize that no one we love ever leaves us while we hold them in our hearts.

Suddenly, a rattling sound from the door brings me fully awake. I bolt upright. Has Bea found me even here? My heart pounds as I reach instinctively for my dog and my hand finds only air.

A moment later, I remember that only Maggie's family and Selena have keys and I put the security chain on. No one can get in.

Then a familiar voice shouts through the letter slot in the door. "Lizzie, I know you're here, and I'm not going away. Please let me in."

Chapter 19

It's Harry, and I can't believe he's here. I glance at my phone. I've been asleep for about three hours. My eyes are swollen with weeping, and I look a complete wreck, but it doesn't matter. Somehow, Harry is here.

"I'm coming," I call down. "Just a minute." I slowly get out of bed, pull a robe on over my pajamas and go downstairs, holding onto the rail as I'm still feeling shaky. When I release the chain and pull open the door, Harry stands silhouetted against the light. Then he steps over the threshold and folds me gently in his arms.

"Oh Lizzie, I've been so worried about you." His voice is full of compassion. "My poor love. Anna got hold of me at the photoshoot and told me what happened. I've been frantic. You weren't answering your phone and I couldn't contact you. I just handed my camera to someone else and left. I just knew you'd come home to Summerfield."

My face is wet with tears again, and I rest my head against his chest. He kisses my hair and strokes the strands from my face as I haltingly tell him what happened.

"Bobby chased Bea when she broke in. I was so angry, but now Bobby's dead because I urged him on. I might as well have killed him myself."

I break away, drowning in tears and sit on the couch, mopping my face with tissues. Harry sits next to me and puts his arm around my shoulders, pulling me closer.

"No, Lizzie, you loved Bobby. You didn't want him to be hurt. He was defending you, and that was his act of love for all you've done for him." He squeezes me tight, and his voice is quiet now. "You were everything to him."

His words calm me a little and Harry reaches along the couch to grab a velvet throw and wraps it around me. He lifts my legs onto the couch and tucks my feet in.

"I'm going to light the fire and make it cozy in here. But first, I'm going to make you some coffee, so lie still and rest."

I lie cocooned on the couch listening to the sound of the kettle boiling and china clinking. I'm so glad he's here, and when he hands me a steaming mug of coffee, I start to feel a little better.

"Now, watch me light this fire. Or not, as the case may be. It was one of my jobs when Sam and I lived here with Mum, but I haven't done it in a long time."

I know Harry is trying to cheer me up as he takes kindling and firelighters from a box next to the hearth.

"Firelighters?" I clear my throat. "Isn't that cheating?"

"It is not. I still do the newspapers the way your granddad, Arthur, showed us."

He rolls sheets of newspaper and knots them like pretzels. He places them in the fire basket, interlaced with firelighters and kindling, making a strong tepee shape, then places three small logs on the top.

"Now, for the moment of truth."

Harry turns to smile at me, and I manage to give him a trembly smile in return. The lighted match touches and flames devour the paper pretzels. Firelighters fizz, kindling catches and a hundred little flames flicker through the tepee. Harry sits back on his heels, well pleased, and reaches to take my hand again.

"We both know from experience that life is often unfair to people and animals that don't deserve the pain." He turns to me. "But Bobby didn't die out on that wasteland, abused and alone. You rescued him, and in a way, he saved your life in return, because that car could have killed you. He should not have died so soon, but he passed away in your arms, surrounded by your love. A lot of people would wish to die like that."

I gaze into the flames and imagine Bobby here beside us, looking up with his dark eyes. His spirit will always be with me, and I'm more at peace now.

"Thank you. It does help to think about it like that." I take a deep breath. "But I can't go back to live in The Warehouse, Harry. It holds too many painful memories now. It was a home for a while, but now I wouldn't feel safe there."

"Well, there is something I've been meaning to tell you." He pulls the throw open and comes underneath it, wrapping us together. He puts his arms around me, and I'm soothed by his special scent of clean skin and herbal shampoo. He's so warm, and I'm in heaven. Then he gives a huge sigh and relaxes, his arms holding me close as we stare into the fire.

"Dad's been trying to sell the land and The Warehouse for years. At Hogmanay, he told me that negotiations were now complete and he's sold the place to a development company for luxury apartments. They're planning a yachting marina as well, which will really turn the area around."

I look up at him. "So, it's not just me? Everyone else will be leaving too?"

Harry nods. "I gave Anna the heads up, and she's already looking for other places. Donal was ready to go too, and Dad says he'll compensate the students for moving out early. So, a lot of change is happening."

"It's certainly been a year for that." We sit in silence together, staring into the fire. A log shifts and sparks fly up the chimney. "I guess you'll just find another crash pad since you're away traveling so much." I look up at his deep blue eyes. He looks soulful, and I feel like I can ask him a question that's been on my mind. "Why do you travel so much?"

He tilts his head to the side as he thinks about his answer.

"You and I both know how divorce impacts a family, but whereas you never saw your dad, Sam and I shuttled between the two halves of our family. Mum was always anxious about money, so Sam and I lived in frugality here and then experienced life in opulence at the castle. I was always confused. Where was home? What is real? Looking through the camera and studying people in different cultures allows me to ask those questions. And I don't put too much trust in romantic relationships, so I tend to stay clear of those."

"But people have always said –"

He gives a quiet laugh. "Yeah, I know. I'm supposed to have a woman in every port, a girlfriend on every photo shoot. I cultivated that myth to stop Mum from matchmaking. There have been one or two wonderful women in my life but not for some time." He looks down at me. "Until you."

His words jolt through me.

"What do you mean?"

He strokes the side of my face with the back of his hand. "For weeks and weeks, I haven't been able to stop thinking about you, and every time I've left, I've wanted to come back to be home next to you. That night at the ball, I wanted to tell you, but then Fiona interrupted us and then the next day, it felt like that dream could never be." He looks down into my eyes and electricity arcs between us. He brushes my lips with his. "Lizzie, you have my heart. I love you. Perhaps I always did, since those days when I'd visit you in the chestnut tree. You're an incredible woman, and I want to come home to you for the rest of my life."

My heart beats faster as he kisses me softly and I want

to lean into him and forget the world outside. It's just Harry and me here together, and for a moment, everything is perfect.

He lifts his head. "Lizzie, would you marry me?"

His words are such a surprise, and they break through my reverie. I've dreamed of him saying them most of my life, but now he's spoken the words, a jolt of fear flashes through me. I pull away from him.

"Think about what you're saying, Harry. You might mean it in the heat of the moment, but you always run away. You've probably booked a flight back to Paris already."

He stands up, his face guilty, and I know my words have hit home. He stares out the window as I continue.

"When I needed help, you weren't there. I was on your list, I know that, but not on the top. You didn't get a deadbolt fixed on my door, and Bea broke in that way. You hurt me, Harry."

He turns, and I see his face in the light of the flickering flames, vulnerable and open. He bites his lip. "I'm so sorry. I've built up this protective shell around my life, but it cracks around you, and I don't know how to deal with it. I have so much to learn, but I need you by my side."

I hug the wrap closer around me. "How can you see the truth through your camera lens, but not what's in front of you?"

He stuffs his hands into the front pockets of his jeans. "You're right. But, Lizzie, you sometimes second-guess me. You make a decision and then move on before I can catch up with you. By the time I get there, you've already gone. And then you blame me."

I nod, realizing that he's right. I have been moving fast, and perhaps my expectations of him were unrealistic.

"You didn't tell me what was going on with Bea," he continues. "Then this happens with Bobby, and you disappear without a word. You didn't tell me where you were going.

Please, please don't do that again, Lizzie. I've tried so hard not to love you, but now I love you so much. I can't live without you."

He takes my hand, and I see the truth in his clear, blue eyes. "We both have our faults, but you know me better than anyone, and I know you too. We would be great together. I'm ready to make that special promise if you'll have me."

It's hard to breathe as I look into his eyes. What do I really want? Because what I say now will take my life in one direction or a completely opposite one.

"I love you, Harry, I always have, and I'm sure I always will. But would our marriage partnership come first for you? Or will you always have a trip booked to Timbuktu or somewhere and leave me behind? Can you put your hand on your heart and say that you wouldn't go? That you'd be there for me?"

His face is serious. "Since you've been living at The Warehouse, all I've wanted is to come home to you. Even when you turn on the hot water in your apartment and I'm hit with freezing cold in my shower." I can't help but giggle at that. "I promise I'll do my part to make our marriage work."

With every kiss and gentle caress, Harry shows me the feelings he's been hiding for so long. "Marry me, Lizzie, and we'll have such fun at the castle. It's a beautiful place in every season of the year. There are wonderful walks, and you'll love it in the snow."

Harry sounds so enthusiastic, but his words hit me like a deluge of icy rain.

"You'll get that huge kitchen and be in charge of all the events that happen in the castle. I know you enjoyed helping Chef when you came up for the ball, and it will be just like those parties your mum had at Home Farm. You'd be in your element."

My heart sinks as I realize that he doesn't see how much

I've changed. My glasses are gone, but in all our talking, back and forth, I've lost sight of my new reality. Harry is destined to be the Laird of a castle in Aberdeen. His wife, like Fiona for Duncan, would need to support him by being responsible for the hotel, organizing the staff and kitchens. A gilded cage, but a cage, nonetheless.

It's a dream come true that Harry loves me, but now I know myself better, and I can't see my home in that future. I move back a little and look up at him again.

"Harry, I love you so much, and I want the best for you. But being the Lady of the Castle, with the Laird as my husband, is not what I want for my life. I want to develop my art. I want a chance to be successful in my own career. I'm heartbroken to say it, but I can't marry you."

Chapter 20

Harry and I stare at each other for a long moment. Neither of us can say anything. My heart pounds and I struggle not to take back my words and fall into his arms. Have I done the right thing?

My phone suddenly pings, breaking the tension. Harry stands up. "I'll make more coffee."

He goes into the kitchen, his shoulders hunched as he walks away. I close my eyes for a moment, gathering my strength. I've been so battered by emotional storms this year; I know I need to make the right choice for me.

I breathe out slowly and then open my eyes again. Sounds of coffee making come from the kitchen, so I check my email and see one from Alex.

Dear Lizzie, Happy New Year!

Your sculpture Head of the Stallion fired success-fully, and the judges' decision was unanimous. It's an outstanding piece of work, and you've been awarded the Academy sculpture prize.

Many congratulations and best wishes,

Alex Johnson, Faculty of Art

I can't help but squeal with excitement. "Oh, my goodness, Harry, I won!"

He comes back through, and I show him the email. He hugs me. "It is a beautiful sculpture. You deserve this success – and every happiness. I wish I could be there next to you."

I see the pain in his blue eyes. "Oh, Harry. Please understand that this isn't a game. I love you and being your wife would be a dream come true. But I can't face a life of service at the Castle, not when my art career is just taking off."

He nods. "It's strange, isn't it, that my mum felt the same when Dad became the Laird. It broke them apart. So I understand how you feel. But promise me you'll tell me when you're hurting, and what's going on with you. I want to be there for you, whatever happens."

I nod and take his hand. "Thank you."

We spend the morning around the cottage together, completely at peace in each other's company. Harry digs out some of the old photo albums from Maggie's attic, and we laugh together to see our early years. I touch the page and stroke Mum's face, alive with energy as she rides one of the stallions. The animals we've had over the years, and some truly terrible haircuts for both of us. An idea starts to form about the next sculpture I want to do as we talk about the future, and I realize that I'm looking forward to going back to Edinburgh for the next step in my journey.

"I have to go back and finish up in Paris tonight," Harry says as we tidy everything away. "Then the family meeting about the estate will be at the weekend." He turns and meets my eyes. "Whatever happens, I'll be back to tell you about it afterward. Please don't run away again without telling me where you are. I worry about you." Like the night of the Highland Ball, that spark of magic is back between us again. He leans down to kiss me gently on the cheek. "I love you, Lizzie. Whatever happens."

Later that day, after he's gone, I look around Maggie's cottage one last time. "Thank you for giving me a sanctuary," I whisper to the old place. It really has been a refuge. As I walk to the gate, a robin sings in the silver birch tree. A hymn of hope for the spring ahead.

* * *

On the train back up to Edinburgh, I work on sketches of Bobby for my next sculpture. I look through all the photographs on my phone. Bobby at the beach, digging holes, chasing seagulls and chewing driftwood he found on the tide line. I begin to sketch his handsome head, the massive paws, and joyful tail. There are so many aspects of his happiness that it's difficult to choose which one to portray. I draw rapidly, channeling my grief into capturing his essence on the page and I smile to see his doggie face come to life again.

I call Anna on the way, and she sounds relieved to hear me cheerful.

"I'm so glad you're coming back. There's good news, too. The Arts Community house has rooms free. It's just around the corner from your college, and I've managed to find a design studio nearby for me because the rooms are too small to work in. I reserved two, in case you wanted to join me for the rest of the year?"

A big grin spreads across my face. "Count me in!"

Back in Edinburgh, Anna picks me up from the train station in a small white car. I give her a monster hug. "How can I ever thank you enough?"

"Make me dinner at the Community House? I've been eating too many take-outs."

"You've got it. Is the car yours?"

She nods. "New Year's gift to myself, now that business has picked up. One of the engineering students went to the car auction with me. It's not new, but he says it has a good engine and I've got transport at long last."

I look out the window as we drive. "And I'm back in glorious Edinburgh. Back to my School of Art, the museums, art galleries, and festivals."

Anna grins. "I told you the place would grow on you!"

But as we leave the city, my heart sinks, because I have to face The Warehouse and Bobby's ashes are waiting there, ready to be scattered. Anna must know how I'm feeling and she glances at me as we drive.

"It's not so bad at the apartment. I had all your stuff moved to the Arts House with mine and Harry had it painted white again."

Once there, we climb the long haul up the stairs, and I pause at the door. The rooms are empty, and the red graffiti is gone. It's a blank canvas once again. I walk to the window and look out across the wasteland, where gigantic diggers are at work, dipping down like dinosaurs feeding. The desolate space will be changed beyond recognition soon enough and the wild bushes where I found Bobby will be gone.

I sigh and turn back to the room. A small wooden box sits on the mantelpiece, *Bobby Martin* engraved on the lid. It's time to take my lovely boy for one last walk.

Anna and I walk together along the estuary beach, just above the incoming tide. I draw deep grooves in the sand, spelling out his name in huge letters. Then I carefully pour Bobby's ashes into the grooves. Anna and I sit with our backs against the breakwater, talking about our happy times with him and as the tide moves softly across the estuary sand, Bobby returns to the elements from which he came.

Later that night, I lie across my bed in the new room at the Arts Community house. Most of my stuff is still in boxes, but I've unpacked my bed things and enough of my art stuff to feel at home.

My phone rings, and it's Harry wanting to know how my

day went. It's strange that he's suddenly so communicative, but it's good to hear his voice and I tell him about the new place.

"Thanks for having the apartment painted. It really helped not to have to read those horrid words again. Anna and I took Bobby's ashes to the beach, and we've done the furniture moving. I start classes again tomorrow."

Harry sighs. "I miss you, Lizzie. I want to come home to you." He sounds tired and depressed. "It feels like so much has changed and moved on. Is there a chance for us?"

I feel a surge of hope but I can't make decisions for him, and he has so many opportunities now. "When's the family meeting?"

"Tomorrow. I'm at Charles de Gaulle airport now waiting for a flight."

"I'll wait to hear from you, then."

All through the following day, I keep glancing at my phone, waiting to hear the result.

But there's nothing from Harry.

Until finally, by the time I'm really getting anxious after dinner, he texts.

Sorry, I just can't call right now. Still thrashing things out. Can you meet me at 81 Huntly Terrace at noon tomorrow? Tell you everything then. H xxx

* * *

Next day, I walk along Huntly Terrace from the bus stop and notice that the snowdrops are now blooming in the front yards. A big black utility van is parked outside number 81, its windows as dark as the paintwork. Harry jumps out as I approach and we hug and hold each other as if we've been apart for years, not days. I'm so happy to see his look of love and feel his excitement.

"What's going on?"

"Walk this way and I'll tell you." He grabs my hand and laughs as he leads me through the gate. "Do you remember that we looked in the windows and around the stable yard, Lizzie?"

He grins, and we climb the front steps. The front door stands open, the old wisteria vine next to it green with new leaves. "The sun is quite warm here on the steps," he says. "Sit with me a minute?"

I sit down next to Harry on the top step with the sunshine on our faces, his leg warm against mine. He takes a deep breath.

"I'm not going to be the next Laird, and I've signed away my legal rights to the Castle." It all comes out in a rush, but he sounds definite – and relieved.

"That's a huge decision to make. Are you sure?"

He nods, his face serious as he holds my hand in both of his. It wasn't what I was expecting, so I squeeze his hand and say nothing, giving him more space to talk. Surely, he can't be doing this for me? Because I don't think that would work out for us, either.

"We had long discussions about everything to do with Dad retiring in March and Jamie is far better suited to be the next Laird. He's been working there all his life. He knows the land, and he's passionate about the estate and the Castle. He'll do a far better job than me. And Heather's going to gradually take over the running of the hotel from Fiona."

Harry pauses, and I want to ask what that means for us. But I just look down at our clasped hands. I must try and focus on where he is right now, not leap ahead of him. "What does that mean for you, Harry?"

"It means I have something to ask you."

Chapter 21

"But you need to come through here first."

He stands and helps me to my feet, then leads me through the front door into the wide hallway. The sun shines through the stained glass window as Harry reaches down into a crate behind the door covered with a Stewart tartan blanket. As he unlatches the door, a tiny black puppy whizzes out and buzzes around the hall in mad circles. I can't help but laugh in delight.

"This is Jazzy." Harry bends to grab the dynamic bundle, and I'm suddenly afraid.

"Harry, she's not for me, is she? I can't have another dog so soon after Bobby."

Harry cradles the puppy as she tries to wash his face with her tongue. "It's okay. She's mine. Besides, she's not really a dog, is she? More like a wee mascot."

He nuzzles her, and she yips with pleasure. I stroke her soft head, so cute with her shiny boot-button eyes, tiny black nose, and triangular ears flapping around. Then around her neck, I see a bright red ribbon with a sparkling diamond ring threaded onto it.

"I'm doing it properly this time." Harry drops to one knee on the floor in front of me, and my heart beats faster.

He holds up Jazzy and the ring all at once. "Would you marry me, Lizzie? I'm going to continue to be a photographer, not a Laird. And I have this bundle of fun to look after too. Please say yes this time and then Jazzy and I are yours forever."

He struggles to untie the ribbon, so I kneel to help him. The wriggling puppy, so soft and adorable, is held between us as she licks both of our faces and I feel my heart opening again. Harry manages to untie the ribbon and puts Jazzy gently on the floor. "Sit, Jazz."

Amazingly, the puppy sits and gazes up at him adoringly. Harry puts a treat on the floor and takes my left hand in both of his. He helps me stand up. My heart is racing.

"Lizzie, I love you more than I ever thought I could love. Please marry me?"

My heart is sure this time. Harry has changed, and this is a future I can see together. "I love you too. Yes, I will marry you – and in my eyes, a photographer is a lot better than a Laird."

Harry carefully slides the beautiful ring onto my finger and leans down to kiss me. I lose myself in him as Jazzy leaps around at our feet, barking with excitement.

Eventually, I pull away. "Are you sure about the Lairdship? You didn't give it up for me, did you?"

He shakes his head. "You gave me the shock of my life at Square Cottage, to be honest. And I needed that kick in the pants. All the way back to Paris I kept asking myself: what do I really want? The answer came back clearly, every time. I'm a photographer by my own choice. I want to create my own path, not inherit something that ties me to a life I didn't choose. I love you, and I want a future with you. This way, we can both do creative work and be together."

"I'm glad you're sure." I look down at the diamond. "And this is beautiful. I love it."

"I hope you'll love this house as well."

He lets go my hand for a moment and calls Jazzy, who is investigating a spider in the corner. He bends his knees, holds out his arms, and she leaps up into them. Then he puts her into her crate and covers it with the blanket to help her sleep while we look around. I marvel at this man who has never settled long enough to care for a dog and now has his own. Things really have changed.

He comes back to me, takes my hand and looks upwards. With its polished wood balustrade, the elegant staircase curves gracefully to the upper floors. "I'd love us to consider this house as a possibility for our future? If you don't like it, we can look at others."

We walk up the stairs. "It's gorgeous, but this would be a massive investment, Harry. Have you got enough money saved?"

He shakes his head. "No, but I told Dad about wanting to marry you, Lizzie, and about this house with stables that we could convert into studios. He's advanced me the money from the sale of The Warehouse. I think it's also my share of the castle, part of me letting that future go."

We stand by one of the big windows with an elegant curve of blue Victorian glass over the top. The walled garden below is a jungle of vegetation and the yard and stable block are run-down and ramshackle. "It's a big project, but just imagine what it could become."

We walk through four enormous double bedrooms, each one with a view toward the city or over the Water of Leith. Harry is enthusiastic in his imagined reconstruction. "The place is big enough for an en suite in our room, then this family bathroom can have a tub and double shower."

He turns the antique faucet, and rusty water drips out. I stoop to pull at twisted old wiring near the bottom of the wall. "The plumbing and electrics would need replacing, and central heating would be expensive for a house this big."

"But essential if we had a young family."

I burst out laughing at his words. "We've only just got engaged, and you're talking about a family already?"

He grins and hugs me, lifting me off my feet to spin me around the room. "I want to make a home with you, Lizzie. So we have to plan for these things."

Back down on the ground floor, we tiptoe across the tiled hall, so as not to wake Jazzy. The huge sitting room has six floor-to-ceiling windows and a solid Victorian sunroom running the full width of the house. Sunlight sparkles through the dusty stained glass, throwing red and blue light across wide, wooden boards.

"What do you think?" Harry asks as we walk out into the yard toward the stables.

"It's totally and utterly fabulous. Obviously in need of tender loving care and buckets of money, but there's a lot of potential."

"We'd have enough money if I budget, and you're great with interior design. It feels like this beautiful house is offering us the chance to bring it back to life." He takes my hands and looks deep into my eyes. "We can make a home, Lizzie. A place we both want to come back to. Could we renovate this place together?"

I look around at the bones of the house and imagine Jazzy running around it, the smell of new paint, colors on the walls and the potential to have a real studio for my art at last. To make a home with Harry would be a dream come true.

I nod. "Yes, my love. I'll make a home with you."

* * *

Our family and friends are delighted to hear about the engagement, and not surprised at all that our long-term friendship has blossomed into love.

"About time," Clair says, as she sends love and congratulations.

There's no hurry to set a date for the wedding, so we concentrate on getting to know each other better and settling into more of a life in Edinburgh. The purchase of 81 Huntly Terrace and the planning applications go through quickly. Harry cancels all his overseas trips, giving the work to fellow photographers. He focuses on local shoots and spends most of his time with builders, plumbers, and electricians. And Jazzy, of course. She loves to walk by the waterside and we even take her back to Bobby's beach. It's good to see her run after the gulls like Bobs used to do, and I can almost think of him without grief now.

Harry sleeps in one of the rooms at Huntly Terrace, keen to work as much as possible while I'm full-on at college, working toward my degree. We spend evenings and weekends together and look over the plans. It's exciting to see the place coming together, and I enjoy sharing my ideas for what our home will become.

One evening over dinner, I show Harry one of the small metal sculptures that have evolved from my initial sketches of Bobby. Welding and metal design are my favorite mediums now. "It's like an addiction. I see shapes and textures so clearly. I think about sculpture all the time."

Harry grins. "I understand completely. That's how I feel about photography. How about we show your sculptures at our first exhibition in the Stables Gallery with my photos of their development and you at work?"

"Oh, that would be fabulous! Especially now I'm studying the sculptures of Andy Scott. Would you come with me on Sunday to look at *The Kelpies*? I'd love to get some inspiration for my next project."

Sundays are always a rest day for us, away from college and building noise at Huntly Terrace. Harry picks me up from the Arts House, and after breakfast at our favorite coffee shop, he drives Jazzy and me to Helix Park. *The Kelpies* are gigantic sculptures of horses' heads, set between the landscape and the sky. I gaze up at them, mesmerized by their power in this natural environment. But now I see beyond the beauty to the structure beneath, and I can see how he would have constructed them.

I point up to the barely visible seams underneath. "It's a fabricated steel structure with stainless steel on top. It must be amazing to create something like that."

"You want to make horses this big?" Harry sounds awed, but a little concerned.

I laugh and hug him. "Not yet. This is Andy Scott's most ambitious project, and it took him eight years. I won't get the chance to do something like this for a while."

But I don't say 'probably never' like I would have said in the past.

Harry and I walk along holding hands, enjoying the fresh air. Jazzy dances ahead of us on her extending lead, intoxicated by all the country smells. Back in the warm front seat of the van, I slide across to Harry. I put my arms around my man, my dear friend, who will soon be my husband. His blue eyes are kind and filled with love as he kisses me. I breathe in the smell of his skin, then I hold his face and kiss him all over it.

"Ahhhh, Stop. Stop, you're tickling me!" Laughing, he fends me off. "Now my face is all wet. You're worse than Jazzy."

Hearing her name, Jazzy leaps into the front seat with one of Harry's expensive camera cloths in her mouth. I try to take it gently from her in exchange for a treat, but she makes growly noises and shakes it like a rat. I lift her onto my lap, stroking her sweet head, and Harry strokes her too.

"She has an enormous personality for someone so small."

Rhythmically, I smooth her coat, and Jazzy calms down. Then her eyelids flutter, and she suddenly falls asleep, as babies do. Harry carefully extricates the cloth, and we drive quietly home.

The following week, Harry schedules a visit to college to take photos of me in my black welding helmet amid the flashing sparks. He does detailed pictures of the four sculptures in progress and then stays on to have pizza with my sculpture group.

"Thanks for coming, everyone, I wanted to introduce Harry."

Alex lifts his soda in a toast. "To Lizzie and Harry. Soon we'll have Lizzie Stewart among us, the newest member of a great Scottish clan."

"Thanks, Alex. I'm truly proud of that, but I'm keeping *Lizzie Martin* for my professional name. Mrs. Elizabeth Stewart will be Harry's wife and live at home."

There's laughter at this because everyone in my class is trying to work out their identity as an emerging artist. Harry admires the *Head of a Stallion*, now exhibited in its spot-lit case. True to what he said at The Warehouse, he arranges with Alex to have it cast in bronze. I'm excited. Not only will I get to see my winning sculpture transformed, but I can watch the whole process at the foundry.

As we leave, Harry takes my hand. "I loved watching you work. You have this concentrated frown on your face, and it's as if the rest of the world ceases to exist."

"I'd love to come and watch you work sometime. I bet you look the same way."

Harry gets out his phone and scrolls down the upcoming shoots. "Of course, this one might be suitable. Remember the shoot I did at Huntly Terrace for an equestrian catalog? The designer needs more images but with a model and horse in fields with an open sky. I scouted and booked a farm just west of Edinburgh. Want a day trip?"

"Sounds great."

* * *

The following week, I join Harry on his shoot. We turn into a lane off the main Edinburgh to Glasgow road and park the van by a farm. A five-bar gate opens onto an empty field with a long, sloping hill, a track to one side and several beautiful trees at the top. Harry points up. "They'll stop it from being too breezy and give a good contrast of light and dappled shade for the various shots."

Harry sets up his cameras with his assistant, and they load up a cart with equipment to take up the hill.

A 4 x 4 arrives, towing a trailer and they park near us. A female groom unloads a big bay gelding with *Dashwood Bounty* embroidered on his immaculate blue saddle blanket. I can't help but take pictures on my phone. He's magnificent. The groom smiles at me as she ties him to the side of the trailer, obviously used to his star attraction.

"Hi, I'm Judith, and this is Dash."

"I'm Lizzie, and he is one spectacular horse. Is he Dashwood Bounty because of Jeff Bounty, the racehorse trainer?"

"Yes, we have a yard of racehorses near Glasgow. Sadly, Dash is not a big winner and doesn't bring in enough at the track, but he earns his keep with modeling." Judith gathers the rest of her grooming kit as Dash moves restlessly. I soothe him, stroking his soft neck while she locks the trailer.

We start up the track just as a limo pulls up next to Harry. The driver leaps out to open the rear door, and a gorgeous-looking woman emerges. She's tall and elegant, wearing fitted jodhpurs over long limbs and a black show jacket with a cloud of amazing dark red hair. She walks over, intimately slides her arm through Harry's, pulls him to her, and kisses him full on the mouth.

"Darling, where have you been all this time? I've missed you."

Chapter 22

I bite my lip to stay silent. I'm sure it's all normal practice at this kind of shoot.

"Melissa, great to see you." Harry extricates himself by bending to pick up a camera case, then waves me over. "This is Lizzie Martin, a student at the Art College. Lizzie, Melissa Perez."

I note that he doesn't mention I'm his fiancée, but we're on his professional turf, so I just smile. "Nice to meet you."

Melissa gives me a hard, bright smile and turns away to greet the people from the equestrian company. She's forgotten me already, and soon enough, she's in the center of a gaggle of makeup and hair assistants as they get ready for the shoot.

The view from the top of the hill is glorious, and Harry soon has everything organized. Dash is on a short leading rein as Judith and I walk over to join them. Melissa stands perfectly poised, her long limbs managing to make the riding outfit super stylish. It would never look like that on me, and to be honest, it's meant to be functional and useful, rather than beautiful. Melissa makes the clothes look good, but she doesn't move around Dash with the experience of a rider.

One of the equestrian company staff hands her a riding helmet, a brand I recognize as one Clair uses in the Stables back in Summerfield. Melissa frowns as she tosses back her red mane and it glints in the sun.

"Darling, we just spent hours getting my hair like this. No way am I squashing it under that ghastly hat-thing."

Judith rolls her eyes at me as I help her take off Dash's blanket. He's polished and image perfect, but bored and irritable. Judith walks him up and down on the short rein and he circles restlessly as the shots are set up. His alert head and ears are magnificent, so I take loads of photos to use for my art projects. The assistant sets up a big lamp with an expanding reflector, and Melissa stands posing before it.

Now Harry is in motion.

Working rapidly, he uses one camera on a tripod and then another from around his neck. His assistant has a clipboard with a list of the shots as Harry focuses on different techniques for when the sun goes behind the clouds. It's fascinating to watch. Melissa is flirting outrageously with him, and although Harry is totally absorbed in his work, he flirts just enough to get her to pose the way he wants. Is that a game played all over the industry, or is there something between them?

I look down the long field and notice that the gate to the road has blown open against the hedge below and a white bag slides over the grass nearby, dropped by the modeling team. The habits of a country girl kick in, and I decide to give myself a break from Melissa, who is now arguing with Harry and Judith about how she should sit up on Dash.

"I can ride, you know. Do the shots with me up on the horse, Harry. Hurry up so we can get out of this filthy place."

I'm grateful to be away from them and I pick up the plastic bag half-way down the hill, before walking down toward the gate to close it.

Suddenly, there are shouts of alarm from the top of the hill.

I turn to see Dash rearing up, Melissa on his back. The lead rein is jerked out of Judith's hand, and Dash is off in a racehorse start. He heads down the hill toward me and the escape of an open gateway beyond.

Melissa screams and pitches forward, throwing her arms tightly around his neck, making him panic and gallop even faster. Beyond the gate, the busy Glasgow road waits at the end of that lane. I can't let them get that far, but I'm not near enough to close the gate in time. Dash's hooves thunder on the earth as he gallops down the hill toward me. I have one chance.

Just before they reach me, I leap into the air and run straight at the horse, screaming and madly flapping the white plastic bag.

I angle to his left side, praying he'll swerve right and away from the gate.

Dash startles, and I see the whites of his eyes as he brakes, front legs outstretched. I jump out of his path and Melissa falls off. Free of her weight, he thunders away, shaking his head and bucking. But he's safe and heads toward the corner of the field where the two hedges meet.

I race down and shut the gate, trying to get my breath back as the team of people hurry down to look after Melissa.

When I get back to them, she is standing, clutching her arm, tears streaming down her face. She curses me horribly, but the ground is soft from the rain, and I know from experience that she can't be badly injured. But the immaculate clothes are filthy, her hair's a mess, and her pride must be horribly bruised.

"I'm sorry, Melissa. But it was the only thing I could do. There's nothing between here and traffic on the main road. You could have both been killed."

Harry hugs me. "Thank you, Lizzie. If you hadn't stopped

them going out the gate …" His look is full of admiration. Melissa's is not, but soon an ambulance arrives, and she's gone.

I help Judith to calm Dash and load him into his trailer, and soon he has his head in a bucket full of horse treats. All is calm again.

Harry is in deep conversation with the equestrian company team and the model agency. He turns at my approach and comes to greet me. "We've heard that Melissa has broken a wrist and is threatening to sue, but it turns out that her group was the last through that gate. They didn't close it after they came in, and there are plenty of witnesses to how she leaped onto Dash's back, startling him that way."

He shakes his head. Whatever the clients say, I shan't be using her again." He straps the big light into a rack in the van. "Now you see why I'm not attracted to models." He bends to kiss me. "I'm so grateful to have you, my love. Can we set a date, Lizzie? I don't want to wait any longer to be married to you."

My heart overflows at his words, because he's right. I don't want to wait any longer, either. Huntly Terrace is almost finished, and I'm ready to be Harry's wife at last.

* * *

The weeks fly by as we get everything organized. Incredibly, Duncan offers to pay for our dream wedding, with a reception at the National Museum of Scotland, one of our favorite places and symbolic of our future in Edinburgh, not north at the Castle.

I take a girls' trip while Harry works at Huntly Terrace one weekend. Anna and I fly to London, then meet Clair off the train from Oxford. We join up with Doreen in Oxford Street and head to the London fabric houses, our phones at the ready to capture pictures of dresses we like. We end up taking mad selfies, talking nonstop and having lunch. It's so fun to be with my two best friends and Anna's mum, who did such a beautiful job for the Hogmanay Ball that I can't imagine anyone else making my dress. Fortified with champagne, we focus on some serious shopping and finally find a store with fabric I love and a pattern to match.

"At last! It's the most beautiful wedding dress I've ever seen. Could you make it, Doreen?"

Doreen puts on her reading glasses to look closely at the pattern I've found. The picture on the front shows a model who looks a bit like me, a petite blonde, with long hair. The dress is strapless and beautifully fitted across the bust, cut from the bodice into a long, paneled skirt. It doesn't have a train but sweeps elegantly to the floor, a little longer at the back than at the front. I show Doreen the white, silk organdie.

"I love that it's such a delicate shade of white with just a touch of pale pink."

Doreen peers at the tiny label. "The design is lace hydrangeas. Yes, I like the soft pink on the edge of the petals. It will look exquisite on you, Lizzie. Harry will see a princess walking toward him."

Chapter 23

On the morning of the wedding, Anna braids the top part of my hair and pins it into a circlet around my head. The rest tumbles over my bare shoulders in long honey-blond curls. Anna and Clair are dressed in their elegant pale silver gowns, and now they help me into my wedding dress. Doreen hand-finished the embroidery, and it is simply exquisite. I really do feel like a princess.

Clair whisks a faint dusting of gold powder across my cheekbones. I grin up at her as she fastens my white-gold necklace. "Can you believe it? I'm marrying Harry Stewart!"

Clair laughs and reaches for Anna's hand. "There's hope for us old maids then!" I know she wishes me every happiness, but I hear the edge of pain in her voice. She broke up with Kyle recently, and I can only hope that she finds someone who is just as right for her as Harry is for me.

Jenna comes in smiling, a bunch of silver and white balloons in her hand decorated with tiny hearts. "You look dazzling, Lizzie. These have just come for you."

Inside the envelope, there's a little silver card with Harry's writing on it.

My darling, Lizzie. Longing to see you very, very soon. I can't wait to be your husband. I love you. H xxxxx (and Jazzy)

I hold the card close in both hands and shut my eyes, imagining him on the way to the Registry Office with Dan right now.

Viv and Maggie come in. "Time to go, Lizzie."

Anna hands Clair and me our posies of spring flowers, and we walk to the stairs. Jenna goes ahead with the balloons, and I walk after her with Anna and Clair as we exit the hotel lobby to smiles and applause from other guests.

At the Edinburgh Central Registry just across the road, Charlie steps forward to stand by my side. I'm trembling as he bends to kiss my cheek. He's come all the way from Australia to be here, and although we still have years to catch up on time together, I'm glad he's here with me today.

"How are you doing?"

"Good, Dad. I think."

We all cross the classical hallway with its marble pillars then walk up the curve of the staircase. I pause with Dad at the top, listening to a piper on the Royal Mile. Then Anna and Clair step forward to swing open the double doors.

I take a deep breath, and we walk on.

Prickles run down my spine to see Harry looking magnificent in his Clan Stewart kilt with full Scottish regalia. He bites his lip as he sees me and wipes his eyes as I walk down the aisle. I try to keep from crying as I walk past family and friends who smile and take pictures. I feel beautiful and special and loved. This truly is a wonderful day.

Harry accepts my hand from Dad with a bow. "Thank you, Charlie. Lizzie, you look simply beautiful."

He leads me forward as Dan and Jamie move next to him, and Clair, Anna, and Jenna stand by my side. Harry lifts my hand and gently kisses the back of it, his blue eyes alight with love. I feel the warmth of his skin and smile up at him as our celebrant steps forward.

"Good afternoon, ladies and gentlemen, and welcome to Lothian Chambers. We are delighted to be here today, to solemnize the marriage of Elizabeth Vivienne Margaret Martin to Harry Duncan Stewart. I am your Registrar today, licensed in Scotland to officiate at the union of Lizzie and Harry."

The celebrant's voice is warm and happy, and she smiles out at our gathered families. "We are here to honor their wish to be together as life partners. If any person here present knows of a legal impediment to this marriage, they should declare it now."

There is a pause, and I wonder whether every bride stands here, worried that someone might speak up. But no one does, and the celebrant goes on.

"Lizzie and Harry, today you exchange vows to love, support and care for each other through both the joys and sorrows of life. Marriage joins two people in a circle of love and commitment to each other. It is both a physical and emotional joining, a promise for a lifetime."

Everyone is perfectly still around us as we speak the sacred words.

"Marriage is voluntarily entered into, a union to the exclusion of all others, so Harry, I ask you first. Will you take Elizabeth to be your lawful, wedded wife, to be loving, faithful and loyal to her for the rest of your lives together?"

Harry freezes and turns to me, his eyes wide with horror. For a moment, my heart pounds. Is he going to run again?

But then he blushes. "I'm sorry, I've forgotten. Am I supposed to say I do or I will?"

A ripple of laughter runs around the room and the celebrant smiles. "It's okay, Harry. You can say either I will, or I do. Shall I read that part again?"

Harry nods and the celebrant asks again, more slowly this time.

Harry takes a deep breath and smiles into my eyes. "I do, Lizzie. I will. Both, all of it, please."

We all laugh and Harry hugs me as I breathe a sigh of relief. It's strange to see my super-confident Harry nervous, but wonderful to know how much this means to him, too. Now the ice is broken, all goes smoothly with my promise and the exchange of our rings.

The celebrant ends the ceremony. "You may now kiss, as husband and wife."

Harry pulls me into his arms, and we kiss to the applause of our family.

We all troop happily outside, into a bright blue day and sunshine. There are no wedding cars because we're only walking a little way along to the Museum for the reception. As the traffic lights turn red, Harry suddenly grabs my hand and pulls me into the middle of the crossroads.

"Trust me, darling?"

All the cars stop as he bends me gently backward over his knee. Our eyes are locked like tango dancers, and I'm held safely in his embrace. We join in a long kiss and the photographers snap some perfect shots with Edinburgh castle in the background.

"Good luck to ye both!"

"Git oot the road!"

There's tooting of horns and good-natured Scottish shouting as Harry carefully lifts me upright again, and we skip across the road to safety. He grins at the photographers with us.

"Great photo opportunity there, guys. Another one coming up."

He pulls the small dagger from the top of his knee sock and offers it to me, handle first as Jenna brings the balloons. "Cut the strings, Lizzie."

Our balloons fly away across the Edinburgh chimney pots, flashing silver and white as they turn in the late afternoon sunshine, higher and higher, disturbing a flock of pigeons swooping in circles until they are lost from sight.

We arrive at the Museum, and Harry and I go up to the roof in the lift with his photographer friend while our guests wait in the grand atrium, chatting, sipping champagne, and nibbling chocolate-covered strawberries.

When we come back in, we gaze down at the floor below us. One end of the marble floor has circular tables covered with crisp, white cloths, cascading flowers and shining glasses. It's incredible to believe that everyone is here for us. Harry holds my hand firmly and we stand together at the top of the stairs. Everyone hushes and looks up at us as we walk slowly down the stairs. My exquisite wedding dress swishes softly around me, and it's so lovely to see all the smiling faces, wishing us all happiness.

The wedding meal is a whirl of tastes and textures, made even more special by the buzz of family and well-wishers around us. After dinner, Harry clears his throat and softly tests the microphone.

"Thank you all. My speech will take up valuable eating and drinking time, so I'll be like the Scottish summer, brief, unpredictable … but hopefully, not too windy."

There's hearty laughter, and I'm glad of it. Harry sounds a wee bit nervous, but I love watching him. My love, my brilliant husband.

"First, my wife and I would like to welcome you to the National Museum of Scotland in beautiful Edinburgh, our home. You've journeyed from far and wide to celebrate with us on our special day. We're blown away to have so many of the people we care about in one beautiful building."

He turns to Maggie, seated with Greg at a top table next to ours with Samantha, Harry's sister, and her husband, Luke, by their side. "I want to start by thanking my mum, Maggie. Thank you for helping me on every step of my journey. You've given me a fascination for life, an appreciation of other cultures, and the education to explore the world. I'm so grateful that you have Greg to share your new life with, too." Maggie beams back at Harry, her eyes brimming with happy tears, as her loving husband, Greg, holds her hand and smiles, too.

Harry turns to Duncan and Fiona, seated on another top table with Jamie, Heather, and Rob. "Thanks to you, Dad, for your generosity and love. For giving us this wedding and for helping us with Huntly Terrace, for helping me to find my own path and make a home for the future."

He raises a glass to Charlie and Angelina, sitting with their children, alongside Dan and Jenna at another table, with Viv and Sid. "Thanks so much to Lizzie's family for all their support. To Charlie and Angelina, for coming all the way from Oz. To Viv and Sid, for all your help over difficult times. To Dan, my best man and now brother-in-law – may there be many more beers to come, mate!" Dan raises his glass in salute. "And, of course, to Jenna, his lovely wife. Our families are now entwined in so many ways."

Then Harry reaches down and takes my hand. "I'd also like to send our love today to Lizzie's mum, Christine. She's too sick to be with us, but she is here in our hearts."

I feel my tears start to fall, as he turns to look at me. "I'd like to speak about the most important person of the day. Lizzie, you look gorgeous every day, but today you are stunning. I'm filled with happiness and so proud to be your husband."

Tears well in my eyes again as he turns to the audience. "I've known Lizzie since we were kids, but I realized how much I loved her at the Hogmanay Ball in Aberdeen. Our love for each other has grown and strengthened through good times, and some tough ones, too." He takes my hand and draws me to my feet beside him. I know I'm blushing, it doesn't matter today. "Lizzie, I want you to know that you mean the world to me. You are my best friend and now my partner for life. I love you so much."

He kisses me softly and then turns to the crowd with a wicked smile. "And now for the second joke of my speech." Jamie lets out a loud Scottish whoop and everyone laughs. Harry grins and soldiers on. "Lizzie and I both like to think we're the boss, but as you can see from what we're wearing, neither of us wears the trousers in this relationship."

Dan boos loudly and there's more laughter. "Thanks for that support from my Best Man!" He lifts his glass. "Please be upstanding to toast the beautiful bride."

Everybody stands and lifts their glasses. "The beautiful bride!"

Harry kisses me again, and we sit down to loud applause. I lean into him. "Thank you, my love. That was a beautiful speech."

"I meant every word of it." Harry wraps his arms around me.

The opening notes of the fiddle start up as a Scottish dance band begins to play. There's a Caller for people who have never done Scottish dancing and music fills the atrium as Harry and I head onto the floor for the first reel. As we spin and jump, we laugh together, then more couples join us on the floor, and we're a whirling mass of happy family faces, linked arms, and laughter.

And suddenly, it's the last dance. What better way to end our wedding than with *Strip the Willow.* Everyone stands in pairs, facing each other in long lines down the floor. We clap in time to the reel, bow, and curtsey, then the top couple, Harry and me, swing each other around. We separate, cross and swing the next person down the line. Back to the center to swing each other again. On and on and on, all the way down the set.

People stamp and cheer as the next top two start the pattern. Then the next and the next, until the floor is a mass of couples swinging each other around. Harry and I arrive at the bottom of the line, breathless, and laughing, arms around each other we watch as our family and friends dance to celebrate our love.

I remember standing on the edge of Jenna and Dan's wedding, watching Harry dance with others. And now, we're here together on a day I will never forget.

After loving farewells, our wedding limo drives us to 81 Huntly Terrace. Harry takes my hand, and we walk up the front steps. The wisteria vine by the front door has burst into cascades of lavender-blue flowers, and it twinkles with fairy lights strung through the branches.

"I love you, Lizzie, " Harry whispers and I turn to put my arms around his neck and kiss him.

"Dearest Harry, I love you, too."

He bends slightly at the knees and sweeps me into his arms, giving me a tender kiss. He carries me across the threshold then, as in a dance, turns us in a slow circle with me in his arms. "Welcome to your new home."

The house is warm around us and it feels familiar, as if we belong here. Harry puts me down gently and pushes the front door shut. We kiss once more in a pool of soft moonlight that shines through the hall window. Then, hand in hand, we climb the stairs.

Harry and me, home at last.

Enjoyed this book?

Thanks for joining Lizzie and Harry in Summerfield and Edinburgh. If you enjoyed the book, a review would be much appreciated as it helps other readers discover the story.

If you want to know when my new sweet romance books are released, you can sign up for my Reader's List here:

www.PennyAppleton.com/signup

More from Penny Appleton

Love, Second Time Around - Maggie and Greg's story

Love Will Find a Way - Jenna and Dan's story

Love, Home at Last - Lizzie and Harry's story

Available now:

Love, Second Time Around

Have you read Maggie and Greg's story?

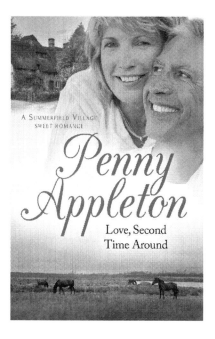

Maggie Stewart is a retired environmentalist, working to preserve the heritage of her little English cottage in Summerfield village. Her children have grown and she's content to ride horses in the countryside and enjoy her retirement.

Except she needs money for her renovations – and she's lonely.

When she joins her old environmental team to go up against an oil company intent on destroying a pristine Scottish river, Maggie finds herself working in opposition to a man she once loved from afar, many years ago.

Idaho ranch owner Greg Warren is rich and entitled, with a dark past that he hides behind a professional smile. But inside, he struggles with loneliness after the loss of his wife and the rage of a wild daughter who won't let him move on.

Love blooms as Maggie and Greg take a chance on a new start, but can they find a balance between the two worlds they inhabit?

In this sweet romance, set between the English countryside and the wide expanse of the Idaho plains, can Maggie and Greg find love second time around?

Available now:

Love Will Find A Way

Have you read Jenna and Dan's story?

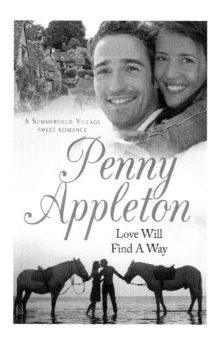

Jenna Warren is an Idaho ranch girl who loves her Appaloosa horse, Blue, and the freedom she has to live her life the way she wants to. But she's increasingly aware that she has never really seen the world, let alone experienced real love, and she hasn't found her purpose.

Daniel Martin is a British schoolteacher, bound by duty to a desperate family situation, and struggling to find his own path as a musician.

When Jenna and Dan meet at a family wedding, they are instantly attracted to each other, but Dan has to leave for Britain the next day. As Jenna follows him back to Summerfield village, a family conflict ignites, tearing their new love apart.

In this sweet romance, set between Idaho and the English countryside, in Japan and tropical Australia, can Jenna and Dan's love find a way through the obstacles that keep them apart?

About Penny Appleton

Penny Appleton is the pen name of a mother and daughter team from the south-west of England. One of us is a *New York Times* and *USA Today* bestselling author in another genre.

We both enjoy traveling and many of the stories contain aspects of our adventures. Some of our favorite romance authors include Danielle Steele and Nora Roberts, plus we love The Thorn Birds by Colleen McCulloch, as well as Jane Austen and Stephenie Meyer.

Our favorite movies include Legends of the Fall, A Room with a View, and The Notebook. We both enjoy walking in nature, and a gin & tonic while watching the sun go down.

We are good friends … although sometimes we want to strangle each other! Family relationships are at the heart of our books.

Sign up to be notified of the next book in the Summerfield Village sweet romance series, as well as reader giveaways:

www.PennyAppleton.com/signup

Connect with me:
Facebook.com/PennyAppletonAuthor
Email: penny@pennyappleton.com

Acknowledgements

Thanks to my proofreaders Liz Dexter
and Arnetta Jackson, and to Jane at JD Smith Design
for the cover design.

Printed in Great Britain
by Amazon